W9-BXA-491

ENTERPRISE™
BROKEN BOW

ENTERPRISE™
BROKEN BOW

A novel by Diane Carey
Based on *Broken Bow*
Written by Rick Berman & Brannon Braga
Created by Rick Berman & Brannon Braga
Based upon STAR TREK created by
Gene Roddenberry

POCKET BOOKS
NEW YORK LONDON TORONTO SYDNEY SINGAPORE

POCKET BOOKS, a division of Simon & Schuster, Inc.
1230 Avenue of the Americas, New York, NY 10020

ISBN: 0-7434-4862-6

First Pocket Books hardcover printing October 2001

10 9 8 7 6 5 4 3 2 1

Printed in the U.S.A.

Parts of this novelization were written aboard the topsail schooner *Pride of Baltimore II* during the American Sail Training Association Great Lakes Tall Ship Challenge of 2001.

D. Carey
Ship's Cook

ENTERPRISE™
BROKEN BOW

PROLOGUE

THERE WAS NO WIND, YET THERE WAS A RUSH. THE STARSHIP was fast, faster than anything, ever. That was the rule. Just from the speed, the bad guys would be too scared to pick a fight. When they saw it go, then, all of a sudden, just magically couldn't see it anymore, they'd know to back off.

Back away, because I'm going. I'm going . . .

". . . where no man has gone before."

Prrrrsssshoooom!

Sure, it was just a paintbrush, but it made the perfect sound, the soft whisk of a starship's superengines, just the way Jonathan heard it in his head, over and over, the way Dad described the sound—the rush of possibilities. Anything could happen! Space—the final frontier!

"Doctor Cochrane would be proud of you," Dad said, instead of *give me the brush before you paint your own nose.*

"I know the whole speech by heart," Jonathan said.

"Watch out! You're painting over the cockpit windows."

Jonathan Archer glanced up at his dad and muttered, "Sorry," and drew back the paintbrush. Before them on the porch table, where Mom hated them to spill anything, was a good reason to spill. The ship was almost finished—a shipbuilder's scale model, one of a kind, because Dad was the builder. Jonathan knew he was the only kid on Earth, in the whole universe and even on Mars Colony, who had a model like this. It was only his because Dad didn't need it anymore, not for planning, anyway.

Jonathan surveyed the ventral plates and complained in his head that the dove-wing paint didn't quite match the gunmetal of the nacelle housings.

But the model wasn't suffering any, except for maybe a little overshoot from his brush on the starboard side. Jonathan was more embarrassed that he might keep the crew from seeing some important thing in space. And let the captain down. Captains had to be able to see everything and know everything. It was the crew's job to help him. *Someday I'll be a heck of a crewman, on this ship! I'll make sure the captain knows everything. He won't take a step without me.*

The boy pressed his lips together and didn't say that out loud. He knew what he wanted, and he would get it. Decision made.

Sunlight poured through the sunporch windows. San Francisco's skyline glittered and enhanced the light shining on the model of the starship. Jonathan was an important person, because otherwise, why would somebody as famous as his father let him work on the actual builder's model of the starship?

*Star*ship . . .

For a few minutes he and his dad were silent as Jonathan

put touches of the darker gray on the featureless white nacelles. He saw his dad's hand twitch, itching to take the brush away and do this himself, but Jonathan leaned closer, signaling that he was determined to be careful and get it right. This was one of those things parents were just croaking to do themselves, but knew they'd be bad kid-raisers if they didn't let their kid try. So Jonathan was ahead. He was almost ten, and he had parents figured out.

"When's it gonna be ready to fly?" he asked his father.

"Let the paint dry first."

"No, I mean *your* ship."

Dad shrugged, but his eyes gleamed. "Not for a while . . . it hasn't even been built yet."

"How big will it be?"

"Pretty big."

Jonathan immediately began weighing comparisons in his head. As big as a Starfleet troop transport? As big as the Universe Planetarium?

"Bigger than Ambassador Pointy's ship?"

Dad opened the can of blue paint and Jonathan dipped the brush.

"His name is Soval," Dad said, "and he's been very helpful, and I've told you not to call him that. Get the leading edge of the nacelle."

Nacelles . . . the magic of faster-than-light drive! Zephram Cochrane's big discovery would take men to the stars—*us*, on our own, without any help from pointers. We had it before they found us, so we could take credit for getting ourselves into space. That was fair. We were coming, and they would have to live with it.

"Billy Cook said we'd be flying at warp five by now if the Vulcans hadn't kept things from us," he dared.

He knew he was venturing into sensitive territory now, but an explorer had to gamble.

"They have their reasons," Dad said, holding back. Then more slipped out. "God knows what they are. . . ."

Jonathan lowered the paintbrush so fast that the stick hit the edge of the table and spat a blue decoration on the ship's stand. He turned sharply, bluntly. "What? What reasons? You always say that! You always say, 'They must have some good reason,' but you never tell me what. I'm ten, and it's time!"

Dad tried not to laugh, then chuckled anyway, and bobbed his brows. "You're nine."

"Nine and three-quarters! If I'm old enough to ask, then I'm old enough to get told something, and not just, 'Well, it's mysterious.' Why won't they help? We would help them! *I* would help!"

Dad's smile faded to something else. He leaned forward, hunched his shoulders, and gazed directly, in a way that made Jonathan feel important.

Then, all at once, Dad started talking—but *really* talking, really saying something, as if he had started speaking to another grown-up all of a sudden.

"I haven't been very fair to you, have I?" he considered. "Treating you the way the Vulcans treat humans . . . the way they've treated me. . . . I've been assuming that I'd be the one to decide when you were ready to know things, assuming you don't have anything to offer because you're . . . you're . . ."

Jonathan flared his arms and spat the word. "Primitive?"

The interruption got just the reaction he wanted. Dad smiled, rolled his eyes, flushed pink in the face, and got embarrassed. For an instant, Jonathan felt as if he looked a lot like his dad—the sun-dipped brown hair, the same brown eyes, pretty good smile that crinkled his eyes, friendly face, not enough of a tan. And the same flicker behind the gaze, like maybe they were both smarter than the next guy about certain things, even if the next guy was each other.

"Primitive . . ." Henry Archer murmured. It was a mocking word, one the Vulcans used a lot, till it was more like a joke.

The sadness in Dad's face, though—it hurt them both. Jonathan shrugged a little, not knowing what to say, but his feelings *were* hurt. His dad had done everything a human could do to prove that we were ready for space, just as good as the Vulcans or whatever slimers were out there, and still the pointers wouldn't teach the important stuff, like they thought we were just puppies in clothes who couldn't learn. They knew how to swim, but wouldn't teach us. They wanted humans to half-drown, like some kind of punishment, then learn to swim on our own, and if we almost drowned, well, then they'd step in, maybe, and be heroes for saving us. What kind of friend is that, to think your friends are less than you in the universe? Some friends. Couldn't they see, just from working with people like Dad and Zephram Cochrane? When Starfleet came around, didn't they get it that we were serious? Didn't they see how much we *wanted* to go? Couldn't *they* learn? Couldn't they *dream?*

So who was primitive, and who wasn't?

If I can make a person like Dad be honest with me, then I can do it with other people, too. I'll think about this later, and figure out what I did right. Then I'm gonna use it on somebody. I'll make the Vulcans talk!

And I'll make them say they're sorry to you, Dad. Because they should be.

As if hearing Jonathan's thoughts, Dad stood up and tapped the lid back on the blue paint. Then he reached for Jonathan's hand.

"Come on, son."

Jonathan took a leaping step, because he knew. "Where're we going?"

"To the Spacedock." Dad drew a long breath and nodded in agreement with himself. "It's time for you to see the real thing."

CHAPTER 1

Thirty Years Later . . .

OKL'HMA!

Failed! I have smashed my craft, and now I flee to live!

Die here? In rows of weeds and seeds? This is no way to die! Suliban! The savage pawns must not have what I know. Escape is not cowardice! Run!

Thus he ran from the smelling wreck of a noble craft that had carried him so far, whose flawed intakes he had not been able to mend in time. The wreck would distract them. It was Klingon to its core and it would serve till the end, spewing a curtain of smoke to hide him in the stalks.

Who was on this planet? Who had made the stalks into rows as tidy as a *mOghklyk*'s spine plait? What beasts were here who built the land into squares, the buildings into squares, and the fences into squares? Were they also square?

Klaang ran, ran like a fear-driven child, but with anger also, which kept him leaping harder with each step. The gravity here—he could run faster than on Qo'noS. His bulky body served better here and seemed young again. He knew he was big, even for a Klingon, but here he sensed an advantage. Suliban animals would lose him in this weed field.

Then the blasts began, and he knew he was wrong. The stalks beside him burst into flame and withered, blackened. A glance over his shoulder told him they were after him even through the smoke and weeds. He saw their mottled faces, heard their weapons, and sensed their insult.

"Hah!" A burst of new energy, driven by the stink of burning plants, drove him faster toward the square buildings he had seen as his craft rushed overhead to its death. A good death in battle for a good old craft, to go ferociously into the dust and flame with scars of Suliban attack. The future would know about it.

The Suliban weapons spat bitter fire at Klaang as he ran. The alien countryside lit up in great expanses. Ridiculously, he tilted toward each shot; escape would be preferred, but if there was no escape, he wanted to die boldly. He was running to save the mission, after all, not himself. His conscience and his duty were in conflict.

But to die with Suliban disruption in the *back*—who would tell how it really had been for him? Why he died with wounds in his back?

Could he run backward?

He was about to try when a port opened in the nearest building and an alien emerged, bright in the face and round in the body, with hairless chin and narrow shoulders and cloth on its head. Shock broke across its expression, and it disappeared back into the swinging port.

Klaang angled away from that building and went for the silver tower to the side. It was windowless and tall, suggesting an inner confusion and a possibility of darkness in which to conceal himself.

The door was large enough for him, made of thin metal and bracings. He pushed it shut and slammed the rod that obviously bolted the door.

Would Suliban be stopped? Klaang stepped back into the darkness and looked at the door. A thin sliver of light around the perimeter proved the door was not tight. Suliban would flatten through it.

He had seen the disgusting sight before. He began to feel his way around, and found a ladder.

By the time he heard the Suliban dislocating their skeletal structure to melt under the door—actually, he heard their shuffles as they reassembled, but in his mind he saw the meltdown—he was bursting out another door, high in the silver tower. Another roof!

Yes, he had seen this nearby small building, and now it was here to help him! He held his breath, and leaped.

His soles slammed onto the tiny roof, breaking the plated material that warded off weather. In his mind, he endured a quick guess about what kind of weather would come to a place like this.

Then he was on the ground again. He lost balance for a moment as he spun around and drew his disruptor. Now! He would get a shot at them! They were inside that port he had just come from, trapped in the metal tower! A disruptor shot would charge those metal walls and force the Suliban out the other end, where Klaang would be waiting for them!

He leveled his disruptor and fired a single salvo at the open portal he had just come from.

Rather than a simple charge, what came out was a gout of sheer fireball. The tower rumbled at its base, then blew to splinters with a great throbbing roar.

Explosives! Why would these aliens keep volatiles in a field of stalks?

Klaang staggered, shocked, blown backward by the unexpected detonation. He stared at the instantly burning wreckage and wondered why a simple tower would get a noble death, just for hiding volatiles.

But the Suliban would have no more interest in him. Not those two Suliban.

"Top ryterr!"

Momentarily confused, Klaang stumbled and turned to see the slope-shouldered alien now standing two steps from him, with a weapon aimed at Klaang's breastplate.

"Aymeenut!" the alien cried.

Klaang tried to make sense of the sounds, which seemed to have some Klingon inflections, but he made much more of the stance. *"Rognuh pagh goH! Mang juH!"*

Would the alien understand his warning?

The alien's face crinkled. *"May'v nodea mityer sning, muttay gerrentee i nowow tuze iss!"*

Why had this creature interfered in the quarrel of others? What kind of people were these? In a rage of insult and irritation, Klaang slapped his thighs and ranted, *"HIch ghaH! Oagh DoO!"*

He was about to spit out his further opinion, when

the alien proved him completely wrong by opening fire.

An energy stream bolted from the weapon and caught Klaang in the chest. As he sailed through the light and bright air to the place where he would die in the stalks, he silently thanked the interesting alien for a wound in front. At least future ages would know he hadn't died running.

CHAPTER 2

Starfleet Spacedock
Earth orbit

SPACEDOCK WAS A TECHNOLOGICAL WONDER. BUILT IN SPACE of geodesic parts assembled on Earth and expanded to full size in space, the shimmering silver dock soared in orbit around a glowing blue planet marbled with white clouds, an image almost religious in its mystical beauty. Within the enormous open structure buzzed a tiny workpod, moving like an insect around the elegant gray-blue body of the planet's first faster-than-light deep-space cruiser.

Together, as the pod maneuvered around the orbital inspection pod and under the rim of a gigantic blue-gray saucer, the two men inside watched through a small ceiling portal as a string of hull bolts breezed past in orderly fashion.

"Well, Trip, ol' boy, it's an unwritten law in these parts that every starship's got to have a country boy on board or it ain't going to fly right."

"You're making fun of me," Engineer Charles Tucker noted.

"Darn right I am, pardner." Captain Jonathan Archer smiled, completely content in the moment. "If I didn't take it out on you, I'd probably go ballistic in the face of some Vulcan dignitary or an admiral or a ship's cook or somebody important."

"Are you saying I'm not important!"

"Why would I say that? You're the country boy."

"Can an engineer tell a captain to shut the heck up?"

"Sure. 'Shut the heck up—' "

"Sir!" they finished together. Their laughter rang through the cramped cockpit. Sounded good. They didn't hurry to stop.

Archer held his gaze on his younger friend a few moments longer than necessary. Tucker was trying to be nonchalant about the new ship's imminent launch, but the veil was thin. He was just as excited as Archer, but Archer didn't feel obliged to hide his near-giddiness at just being here, skimming across this ship, at this time in history. The two weren't quite nine years apart in age, and between Archer's boyishness and Tucker's pretending to be a grown-up at least half the time, Archer figured that put them pretty close. Of all the newly assigned crew, they'd been together the longest, from the design stage to fitting-out of the new warp-speed ship. The new ship hovered above them in Spacedock, as comfortable as an eagle in its aerie, being tended, coddled, and preened by devoted minions in extravehicular suits, none quite as consumed with wonder as the proud captain himself.

"I wish Dad could've seen this. . . ."

At his side, Tucker let his bright grin soften to a misty

understanding. "Everybody does, John. Some things just aren't gonna come out fair. I don't think anybody in Starfleet'll ever quite forgive the Vulcans for stalling."

"The worst part is how they pretend they didn't," Archer commented drably, "as if we're too silly to know the difference. I've been waiting thirty years for them to open up, and it's never really happened. They just keep dangling that carrot."

With one hand on the helm controls, Tucker held out the other palm and said, "But look what we've done anyway. There she is!"

Archer smiled, heartened, and drew a deep breath. "Yes, there she is. . . ." He gazed for a moment at the underbelly of the meaty, stubborn-looking ship's wide saucer section, then turned a grateful regard to Tucker. "With you around, who needs a ship's doctor?"

"We do." Tucker whirled the inspection pod around sharply as they came to the neck section and speared downward toward the nacelles. Beneath, the planet Earth gleamed mightily in a sheen of sunlight that made Spacedock glitter. The old Earth and the new ship moved together through the solar system that had given them both life. Magic!

"The ventral plating team says they'll be done in about three days," Tucker offered when he saw where Archer's eyes were leading.

"Make sure they match the color to the nacelle housings."

"Planning to sit on the hull and pose for postcards?"

"Maybe." Archer smiled again, and sighed happily. "God, she's beautiful. . . ."

"And fast! Warp four point five on Thursday!"

Archer shivered with awe. "Neptune and back in six minutes! Let's take a look at the lateral sensor array."

Before the last syllable was out, the pod vectored ninety degrees on its port seam and spun aft, dropping fifty feet like a stone. Only at the last second did Tucker wheel out of the fall.

Archer closed his eyes and swallowed a moan. These stupid utility pods—smaller than they had to be, and definitely faster than they had to be.

"If I didn't know better," Tucker chided, "I'd say you were afraid of flying."

"If I'm afraid of anything," Archer said, "it's the scrambled eggs I had for breakfast."

"Pretty soon, you'll be dreaming about scrambled eggs. I hear the new resequenced protein isn't much of an improvement."

Archer skewered him with a meaningful look. "My number one staffing priority was finding the right cook. I think you'll be impressed."

"Your galley's more important to you than your warp core. That's a real confidence builder!"

"You're a great engineer, Trip, but a starship runs on its stomach. Slow down—there. Those are the ports that buckled during the last test. They need to be reinforced."

Tucker released the controls, picked up a padd and a stylus, and scribbled notes to himself, checking the numbers on the hull plates and poking the identifiers on a schematic of the section that came up on his padd. With one passion competing with another, the pod drifted sideways and—

Ponk—struck the body of the new ship, then made a lazy yaw to starboard.

"Sorry . . ." Tucker kneed the controls and the pod stiffened to a more stable position.

Archer pressed forward in his seat and craned to look out the viewport. "Great. You scratched the paint."

Tucker took a breath to make his presence known, but the com chirped and cut him off. He tapped the button. "Orbital Six."

"Captain Archer? Sir?"

Oh, well, they'd found him. Arched leaned back. "Go ahead."

"Admiral Forrest needs you at Starfleet Medical right away."

He looked at Tucker, but the engineer just shrugged.

"Very well," Archer called to the com. "Ask him to stand by. I'm on my way."

"Thank you, sir."

Tucker was still looking at him, even though he was also now spinning the pod out of the presence of Spacedock and heading toward the planet. "Who's sick?"

Archer shrugged. "It can't be personal. Everybody I care about is up here."

"Come on, John," Tucker sighed. "Don't be bitter. Not today."

"Don't worry, I'm not. It's just the truth. A little truth never—"

"You and the truth. Can't we have a little old-fashioned social disguise from our captain? Fool us some? Lull us into complacency?"

Archer laughed again and dropped a hand on the engineer's arm. "Tucker, you are *plenty* complacent enough! Speed up, will you?"

"But the approach vector limit here is—"

"They can give me a ticket. Whatever Forrest's got, I want to get it over with and get back here while the getting's good."

"That's a lot of 'gettin,' Captain. I'm on it! Hang on!"

"Trip! Holy—!"

"Who was chasing him?"

"We don't know. They were incinerated in the methane explosion, and the farmer's description was vague at best."

"How did they get here? What kind of ship?"

"They were using stealth technology. We're still analyzing our sensor logs."

"I'd like to see those logs."

"The Klingons made it very clear. They want *us* to expedite this."

"It happened on *our* soil."

"That's irrelevant."

"Ambassador, with all due respect, we have a right to know what's going on here!"

"You'll be apprised of all pertinent information."

"And just who gets to decide what's pertinent?"

Jonathan Archer knew exactly what was going on before he ever entered the ICU at Starfleet Medical. There were five voices—Admiral Forrest and that other funny little admiral who always reminded him of Grandpa's golf partner . . . Admiral Leonard was his name. Commander Williams as well. The other two—well, he knew Ambassador Soval's voice well enough, curse him, and the other was clearly a Vulcan, too. That snooty tone of voice, the precise diction, and the shield of parentlike solemnity—Archer almost made an unpleasant sound, but decided to just walk in instead. Probably the same effect.

He was still in civilian clothes, but he didn't care. If they wanted formal, they could invite him to a dinner party, not demand that he interrupt his shakedown inspection to visit a sick—

What the hell was that?

Big, that's what. And noticeably hairy. And toothy. The massive humanoid form was hooked up to just about every contraption this place had to offer. Life support? Was it dead?

"Admiral," he spoke directly to Forrest and made eye contact with the other two humans, deliberately leaving out the two Vulcans, who now gazed at him with mixed disapproval.

"John, I think you know everyone," Forrest mentioned, whether it was true or not.

"Not everyone." Archer studied the big sick guy through the isolation window.

Admiral Leonard tried to help. "He's a Kling-ott."

"A Kling*on*," one of the Vulcans corrected.

Archer looked at the Vulcan, picking up an underlying joy in correcting a human admiral. Now he remembered this one. Ambassador Tog? Tos?

He started to say something, possibly rude, when a movement behind the two Vulcans caught his eye. Another Vulcan. A woman. Wasn't anybody going to introduce her? Or were the Vulcans so advanced that courtesy didn't involve women?

He decided their protocol was their own problem, and put his attention back with the Kling-On.

"Where'd he come from?"

"Oklahoma."

"Tulsa, right?" Archer moved closer to the glass.

"A wheat farmer named Moore shot him with a plasma rifle," Forrest filled in. "Says it was self-defense."

"Fortunately," Tos added, "Soval and I have maintained close contact with Qo'noS since the incident occurred."

Archer turned. Oh, what the heck—just ask. "Qo'noS?"

"It's the Klingon homeworld," Admiral Leonard said, proud that he could pronounce it now.

Forrest eagerly added, "This gentleman is some kind of courier. Evidently, he was carrying crucial information back to his people—"

"When he was nearly killed by your 'farmer,' " Soval stuck in.

Uh-oh. Archer's back stiffened. He knew that tone, that inference. *Your farmer.* Good thing he was well enough educated to understand the subtle nastiness as wielded by the pointy among us.

He turned, faced them all, tilted his head just a little, and waited for the other shoe to drop.

Carefully Admiral Forrest finally admitted, "Ambassador Soval thinks it would be best if we push back your launch until we've cleared this up—"

"Well, isn't that a surprise?" Archer snapped. He looked directly at Soval with what he hoped were his father's eyes. "You'd think they'd come up with something a little more imaginative this time."

Soval's face was impassive. "Captain, the last thing your people need is to make an enemy of the Klingon Empire."

"If we hadn't convinced them," Tos filled in, "to let us

take Klaang's corpse back to Qo'noS, Earth would most likely be facing a squadron of warbirds by the end of—"

"Corpse?" Archer broke in. "Is he dead?"

That would change things, but he had no idea how. What was an alien agent or courier doing bumbling about on Earth anyway? If Archer understood the general layout of this part of the galaxy, Earth wasn't particularly easy to stumble onto, which was why nobody had stumbled here until Zephram Cochrane sent up his big flare.

The Vulcans were annoyed at his questions, but Archer wasn't about to be swayed by that. Where was it written that humans had to be polite and accommodating to Vulcans and everybody else, but nobody felt obliged to be polite back?

Starting today—

He stepped past Soval and Admiral Leonard to the ICU door, opened it, and cued a passing physician. "Excuse me—is that man dead?"

Though in hospital garb, the physician was some kind of exotic alien breed, nothing Archer recognized, but his delight at getting to work on this patient was downright human. "His autonomic system was disrupted by the blast, but his redundant neural functions are still intact, which—"

"Is he *going* to die?" Archer pestered. Yes or no. Just yes or no.

"Not necessarily."

Close enough.

Without amenity, Archer turned back to the five musketeers. "Let me get this straight. You're going to disconnect him from life support, even though he could recover. Where's the logic in that?"

"Klaang's culture finds honor in death," Soval explained. "If they saw him like this, he'd be disgraced."

"They're a warrior race," the other Vulcan went on. Did these two always share lines? "They dream of dying in battle. If you understood the complexities of interstellar diplomacy, you would—"

"So your diplomatic solution is to do what they tell you? Pull the plug?" Archer heard his temper rising in his tone. Why not? The putrid lesson in diplomacy betrayed the Vulcans' own ignorance. What Earthling hadn't heard about a dozen cultures on his own planet with that Viking morality of dying in battle? It wasn't exactly new, and Earth was only one planet. So the Klingons carried it to an extreme—all it did was guarantee that they'd be at war with somebody all the time and they'd fight each other if they couldn't find some stranger to fight. And the Vulcans called Humans primitive? But this they respected?

"Your metaphor is crude, but accurate," Tos said.

"We may be crude, but we're not murderers." Archer turned a cold shoulder to the Vulcans and faced Forrest. "You're not going to let them do this, are you?"

And he asked in a way that made them all understand that *he* wasn't going to let this happen and the admirals could help if they wanted to. As he waited for their decision—whether to agree with him now or in a few minutes—he glanced at the enormous form on the ICU bed, its legs hanging off the bed from the calves on down. This Klingon hadn't even had the chance to die in battle. He'd crashed and was running. What kind of battle death was that? Better he live and pick something better.

Maybe a hand-to-hand with Tucker. Or Soval. Yeah . . .

Soval leaned a little toward them. "The Klingons have demanded we return Klaang immediately."

"Admiral?" Archer prodded, ignoring the ambassador.

Forrest fidgeted. The sight enraged Archer. That the Vulcans and Klingons could reduce a Starfleet admiral to nervousness—some things just shouldn't happen. It was time they stopped happening.

"We may . . . need to defer to their judgment," Forrest attempting, trying to make everybody happy.

Boy, was it ever time for this guy to retire. Brave new world, that has such marshmallows in it.

"We've deferred to their judgment for a hundred years," Archer snapped.

"John—"

"How much longer?"

His bluntness did the trick, not to mention the clarification that he really wanted an answer. This wasn't rhetorical. He was making a demand not for himself, not for Klaang or the new ship, but for Earth, to establish itself a stake separate from the Vulcans. If they wouldn't come up to the plate, Earth would come up without them. Archer was ready. Why weren't these others? When would there be a better chance to demonstrate what humanity was all about, among these people who thought silly things were important? How you died instead of how you lived, for instance.

The Vulcan female stepped forward, quite suddenly, right through the two elder ambassadors. She was the only one with the guts to say what she was thinking.

"Until you've proven you're ready."

Archer bristled. The Vulcans kept chanting that mantra, but they were never interested in letting Earth people do anything that might just prove readiness. Who did these stiffs think they were anyway? Interstellar schoolmarms?

"Ready for what?" Archer asked, even though he knew. Hell, everybody knew, but he wanted to make her say it.

"To look beyond your provincial attitudes and volatile nature." The elegant female had a firmness in her eyes. She was playing his game. She darn well comprehended the triteness of her own declaration. Maybe she was waiting to see how far Archer could be pushed.

"Volatile?" Archer mocked with a little lilt. "You have no idea how much I'm restraining myself from knocking you on your ass."

Eyebrow raised, she looked at him in near enjoyment—was that right? There was a glint in her eye, despite her mosaic stillness. He got the idea she might not like what she heard, but did like hearing it. Very few humans talked back to Vulcans . . . yet.

I think I'll start doing seminars. "How to Talk Back to a Vulcan and Spit in an Admiral's Eye 101. You, too, can learn this in ten easy lessons."

Oh, forget it. He pivoted back to Forrest. "These Klingons are anxious to get their man back. Fine. I can have my ship ready to go in three days. We'll take him home. Alive."

"This is no time," Soval interrupted, "to be imposing your ethical beliefs on another culture."

Archer just cast him a look of deadly irony, and waited while Forrest turned to Leonard.

"Dan?" Forrest asked.

"What about your crew?" Leonard asked. "Your com officer's in Brazil, you haven't selected a medical—"

"Three days. That's all I need."

Okay, everybody always said "Three days," so Archer had picked it out of a hat, hoping they'd think it had a good ring.

"Admiral," Soval protested. No doubt he was having nightmares about a crew full of Neanderthals shooting through space into "civilized" areas like the Klingon cul-de-sac.

"We've been waiting nearly a century, Ambassador," Forrest said at last. "This seems as good a time as any to get started."

"Listen to me," said Soval, his voice noticeably louder. "You're making a mistake."

Archer's reply was calm, but there was no mistaking the condescension. "When your logic doesn't work, you raise your voice? You *have* been on Earth too long."

The debate was over. Forrest had found what might be his last tidbit of resolve and made a decision. Archer tried not to puff up too much. Not *too* much.

The female was watching him. Well, maybe puff a little more.

Oh—there they went. The renowned ultrasophisticated civilized nonprimitive Vulcan turn-and-stalk-in-a-huff. Archer almost smiled, but managed to bury it. Score one for the amoebas.

Forrest waited until they were gone, then winked at Leonard and spoke to Archer. "I had a feeling their approach wouldn't sit too well with you, John. Don't screw this up."

Archer restrained his comment. The last part must be meant as a joke, because nobody would say it to a captain and be serious. Maybe Forrest had invited him here just to provoke this very outcome. Possible? Was there some deck officer in the old boy yet? Better give him the benefit of all doubts and not fiddle with success.

Archer just smiled and pretended to get all messages.

As Forrest, Leonard, and the rather bewildered Williams exited the ICU window chamber, muttering a discreet continuation of the whole argument, Archer moved to the glass partition and rapped a knuckle on the window. The alien physician and a couple of nurses flinched, looked at the equipment, then noticed Archer motioning.

He gestured to the alien. *Psst. Come here.*

The young alien paused. *Me?*

The labyrinth glowed dimly with mysteries and technology provided by even more mysterious presences. The room was bisected by a huge archway that contained unexplained energies, a rippling barrier between here and elsewhere, unidentified, a crossroads between the concrete here and the vague there.

Silik stood on one side, in the here, at the podium that sent pulses of energy through the archway to identify him. He was Suliban, a senior of the Cabal, here reduced to childhood by the being who floated on the other side of the archway. The creature there was as unidentified as the place from which he broadcast himself. They were a mere arm's length away, but they were separated by the ages. Silik felt the privilege of his position eaten up by the smallness of his power.

"Where's Klaang?" the milky being in the portal spoke. There was a preecho that obscured the creature's words. Even his form was obscure, though he had a head and arms and legs like Silik, like most of the creatures who had achieved intelligence in this galaxy. But perhaps that creature wasn't in this galaxy. Anything could be true, and Silik was at this person's disposal for facts or deceptions. As he stood here, a lifetime's achievements in the Suliban Helix were subordinated to this glowing individual beyond the archway.

"The humans have him," Silik provided bluntly.

"Did you lose anyone else?"

"Two of my soldiers were killed." His jaw grated tight at this report. "One of them was a friend. Can you prevent it?"

Coldly, the creature said, "Our agreement doesn't provide for correcting mistakes. Recover the evidence."

The preecho was both intoxicating and maddening. These ghostlike creatures had all the advantages. They had technology, which they dangled before the Suliban, a chance for enhancements far beyond the foreseeable future of technology. They wanted to tamper with things. The Suliban were their conduit. Silik wanted what they could give, but he disliked catering so much to them without any return of respect.

What choice did he have? They had all the power, and all of time on their side.

"I will," Silik said. "I promise you. When will we speak again?"

The figure beyond the archway seemed to enjoy this part of their conversation whenever it came. He liked speaking of time as a plaything, as his pet. Silik could only stand by and be told yet again what he had heard before.

"Don't be concerned with when," the ghost said.

And the creature vanished, without the slightest hint of ceremony. The radiant energy subsided to a simple haze. The archway disappeared.

Once again Silik was alone in the labyrinth, thinking about losses and gains, and wondering which the Suliban would have in the end.

CHAPTER 3

"MR. MAYWEATHER, DON'T STAND TOO CLOSE TO THAT contraption, please, lest we lose a bit of you."

"Don't worry, Mr. Reed. I'll be tending all the bits of me."

"Mmm . . . to be sure. New technology is always perfect from the start."

Malcolm Reed held his concern in check, but was quite prepared to drop his Lord Nelson persona and knock Travis Mayweather right off that platform if any bit began to sparkle. Such a nightmarish miracle, this. "All right, now you really must stand clear. We're receiving a clearance to—what's the word they decided upon? Ream?"

"Beam." Mayweather's cocoa complexion glowed a little in the overhead prism lights that would soon show themselves as more than conveniences.

"Amazing, the group dynamics assessments they undertake to select descriptive terms for the unimaginable."

"I heard they went through 'scramble,' 'heat,' 'dissemble' and 'spear,' before they found one that wouldn't scare people. 'Beam' sounds so peaceful and sunny—"

"Not quite what's going on here, is it?" Reed sighed at the awesome complexity of this contraption.

Travis Mayweather, though, was giddy with pleasure at the new might of their science. He had just come aboard, and the glaze of awe had yet to take a scuff. It would be his privilege to be the first command watch helmsman of this ship, and he knew his name would probably go down in a few history books. Reed contained his approval with proper British reins, but was secretly pleased at a shipmate's delight and fulfillment.

Mayweather looked particularly stylish in the Starfleet dark-blue jumpsuit, with its geometrically drawn shoulder piping. Reed liked the uniform design. Simple, comfortable, easy on the eye, yet just military enough to make everyone stand properly. He wished they would bring back hats.

In any case, soon they would all be fulfilled, for they were all privileged. As armory officer, Reed's duties would be rather less glamorous than Mayweather's, but had the potential to be more satisfying in the large picture. Ah, well, time would tell whose stories might live on. Until then, it was their charge to make this interesting gadget functional to their purposes.

He stepped to the control island and flipped a toggle.

"Very well, dockmaster, we're ready for you to engage the transporter."

"Roger, shipboard. Are you standing clear of the platform?"

Reed glanced at Mayweather, who backed up two more steps and shrugged. "That's affirmative." He, too, stepped back, but commented, "Either this gentleman is paranoid or psychic. Both useful traits, I should imagine."

The hairs on his skin began to shiver even before the lights on the platform changed. The transporter chamber quickly became a receptacle of patterns and flashes that made Reed wish there were some kind of partition to protect them. This thing *must* be giving off some kind of ray or contaminants. How else could it work? So much scrambling energy simply had to radiate.

But they said it didn't. The royal "They."

He and Mayweather watched, each guarding his expression, as containers of various sizes formed inside the chamber, bathed in glitter and fanfared by an earsplitting whine.

"Let's hope something's done about that squawk," Mayweather commented over the noise.

"I shall send a memo." Reed glanced about and scanned the control island after the whine had stopped and the lights had faded. He didn't really believe it was completely safe to stand up there. What if someone hit the wrong button on the other end?

He controlled his apprehensions and led the way onto the platform, which now contained a clutter of cargo kegs that moments ago had been miles away. Despite the skittishness of the contraption and the doubtful nature of its methods, the transporter was indeed a magical gift from humanity to itself, a fulfillment of dreams from travelers from ages untold. To wish to be there . . . then to *be* there . . .

"I heard this platform's been approved for biotransport," Mayweather said as he pushed the receiving authorizations on the side of each container.

"I presume you mean fruits and vegetables," Reed drawled.

"I mean armory officers and helmsmen!"

Reed accommodated him by touching his own uniform front with an expression that said *Moi?* "I don't think I'm quite ready to have my molecules compressed into a data stream."

"They claim it's safe."

"Do they indeed . . . well, I certainly hope the captain doesn't plan on making us use it."

"Don't worry. From what I'm told, he wouldn't even put his dog through that thing."

Reed opened a canister and was engulfed in frustration that changed the subject. "This is ridiculous. I asked for plasma coils. They sent me a case of valve sealant. There's no chance I can have the weapons on-line in three days."

"We're just taking a sick man back to his homeworld. Why do we need weapons?"

"Didn't you read the profile on these Klingons? Apparently they sharpen their teeth before they go into battle."

Mayweather shrugged. "Then don't let them get close enough to bite you."

"Personally," Reed opined, "I suspect it's all rubbish and lore. After all, with whom do they do all this battling they speak of? And who supports this constant tactical front? Someone must do the sewing, cooking, construction, repair, and run a supply line, correct? Someone must cobble the soldiers' boots, as they say. One should think they must have some other flammable race which also prefers to battle constantly, or they would have to simply battle with everyone they meet.

Sooner or later, someone will have shown them their own heads."

"You really think it's a myth?"

"Oh, yes. One simply can't behave that way without ultimately coming up against a bigger dog, sharpened teeth or no."

"And a more disciplined dog, sir?"

"Why, of course. Discipline ultimately beats all Celts and Huns. It's the British way."

Mayweather rewarded him with a stream of laughter as they exited the mystical transporter room and hurried down the corridor, through a scaffold of working crewmen engaged in the hustle of making the ship ready in record time. No one had been ready for the captain's morning muster. Three days? They wouldn't be ready, but there would be a passable pretense of readiness.

"No doubt Mr. Tucker will reassure me that my equipment will be here tomorrow," Reed went on, satisfied with his performance for the day. He continued, imitating Trip Tucker's Southern drawl. "Keep your shirt on, looo-tenant."

Mayweather wasn't listening. "Is it me or does the artificial gravity seem heavy?"

Reed took a few measured steps. "Feels all right . . . Earth sea level."

"My father always kept it at point-eight G. He thought it put a little spring in his step."

"After being raised on cargo ships, it must've felt like you had lead in your boots when you got to Earth."

"Took some getting used to—"

"Excuse me." Though Mayweather took a breath to say more, Reed was on to something else, for he had spotted a crewman about to tune the power conduits to the lower levels with his magnetic coil reader. "You may find that if you rebalance the polarities, you'll get that done quite a bit faster, crewman."

The midshipman glanced at him.

"Thank you, sir," the young lady said, not meaning it.

"Very well. Come along, Mr. Mayweather."

As the two men continued hurrying down the corridor, Mayweather cast a glance back and chided, "What was that all about? She didn't need the help, y'know. Did you enjoy a little venture into superiorizing?"

"Yes, I did. Of course, it also helps that everyone in earshot got a little jab that we are indeed in a genuine hurry."

"Ulterior motives. Sneaky."

"Anything for king and country."

"Listen, Malcolm," Mayweather began, more quietly, "If I didn't thank you for recommending me for this assignment, let me do it right now."

"Oh, all I did was drop a syllable or two into the captain's ear. Your record spoke for itself. All your life aboard spaceships, able to fly nearly any make or model—"

"There's no model like this one."

"No, there isn't. So take heart, for there's nothing against which to compare you. No one will know whether you're mucking up at the helm or not. Wait—engineering is *this* way. Always bear to starboard below deck eight."

"Starboard, aye. But thanks anyway."

Reed nodded. "We shall see."

"Okay, Alex, give it some juice!"

Trip Tucker danced his own kind of ballet through the

outcroppings and knotholes of the cramped engineering deck, a complex scaffold made to support experimental technology of the most skittish kind. This was the red-light nerve center of the new ship, busy and tightly fitted, a place where a thousand adjustments had been bolted on where they were needed, from circuit breakers to flow quenchers, some just to see if they helped at all. Tucker swung and dropped, hooked and monkeyed through the arrangement rather like a child on playground equipment or a zoo monkey on the run. Malcolm Reed winced as Tucker's foot slid on a rung, but the engineer succeeded in barely keeping a heel-hold with the other foot and hovered in place to check whatever he was doing.

"Beautiful!" he cried to someone among the many crewmen rushing around this area. "Lock it off right there!"

His voice, so high against the chamber's ceiling, carried an echo. Reed, with Mayweather at his side, stood watching Tucker in his engineering flight suit dance about the ladders and support structures for the mighty and prelegendary warp core. Yes, the massive shipborne power plant already was a legend across space—the clever, useful, and somewhat shocking development, all-human, in spite of holdbacks from other races who already had faster-than-light speed. Apparently humanity had surprised everybody, coming up with warp power on their own, then developing it so quickly. For other cultures, it had taken centuries to get from point A to point B in this technology, but once humans had seen what others could do and knew they could do it, they wouldn't be left behind now that they had a grip on the possibility. When the Vulcans held back, humans had surged forward with even harsher relentlessness. Spite? Perhaps, and wasn't it joyfully irritating?

"Look at him," Reed commented. "The very embodiment of glee."

"I would be, too," Mayweather sighed, "if this baby were all mine the way it belongs to its chief engineer."

"Oh, or its primary watch helmsman, I dare say. Don't sell your role short. You are the first, after all."

"You're determined to make me self-aware at the wheel." A bright smile broke within Mayweather's face. "But you're right—it's giving me butterflies to realize what I am, and where I am. Do you think all the men who came before us on ships felt like this?"

"Unless they were shanghaied." Reed muttered his comment, then realized he had failed to fan the mystique. "Ah," he added, "but each age has its *Enterprise* . . . and always has. This is ours, for all our own people, and any other who wishes our friendly hand."

Mayweather accepted the heartfelt sentiment. "Or our firm fist."

"Amen to that."

The two stood together, in their ship, among shipmates, and embraced this moment of charm.

A dash of spritely humanity came as Trip Tucker swung downward toward them, finally to slide down the handrail of the last ladder and land with a thunk on the deck not ten steps away, proudly eyeing the warp core. At last he pulled out an engineer's cloth and relieved a smudge of its misery.

"I believe you missed a spot," Reed charged.

Tucker turned, and seemed immediately proud, then eyed Mayweather.

"Commander Tucker," Reed introduced, "Ensign Travis Mayweather."

Tucker stuck out his hand eagerly. "Our space boomer!"

Mayweather seized the hand and tried to return the enthusiasm—helmsman and engineer, the right and left hands of any ship—but he couldn't keep his eyes off the stunning warp core.

"How fast have you gotten her?" he asked, finding a compromise that excited them both.

"Warp four! We'll be going to four point five as soon as we clear Jupiter. Think you can handle it?"

Reed buried a grin at the two children who had found each other in the midst of fantasyland, each wanting to do the other's job, just for a few minutes.

"Four point five . . ." Mayweather gazed hungrily at the power source, openly awed and not ashamed to show it. Unthinkable speed, indescribable power, soon to be in his hands.

"Pardon me," Reed interrupted, "but if I don't realign the deflector, the first grain of space dust we come across will blow a hole though this ship the size of your fist."

Tucker snapped back to business. "Keep your shirt on, Lieutenant. Your equipment will be here in the morning."

"What's taking so long?"

"There was some problem at central dispatch with Spacecrate Incorporated's shipment manifest. The crate with your stuff in it got waylaid in transit, and it's being rerouted."

"By whom? Who signed that reroute order?"

"Some guy at the dockmaster's office."

"Seems odd . . ."

"That's what we get for trying to hurry things up—they get more late."

"But the shipment was confirmed for this afternoon," Reed protested. "I got the bill of lading. How do these things occur? Inefficiency?"

Tucker shrugged. "We've had six foul-ups already, and it's not even breakfast. You're not the only one."

"All involving shipments?" Travis Mayweather asked.

"All but two, which were misinstallations of critical parts for the motive power system. I'm having to watch my engineers like a mama lion."

Reed frowned. "Who made these misinstallations?"

"Don't know. We're trying to trace them, but nobody seems to know where the work orders are coming from. Just confusion, is what I think."

"Well, I don't care for that at all . . . where's the captain?"

"Oh, him?" Tucker shrugged again. "Where would you be if you had just ordered your ship fitted out with a seventy-two-hour readiness deadline and you didn't even have a deflector or a command staff? He's in Brazil. Where else?"

"Ghlungit! tak nekleet."

"Very good. Again."

"Ghlungit! tak nekleet."

Ah, the sound of learning. Jonathan Archer came up on the doorway of his target classroom and noticed that he'd been doing a lot of eavesdropping lately. Gotten a lot of information out of it, too. He paused for a couple of moments and listened, trying to pick out which language the students were repeating to their teacher. The process was heartwarming, but quickly becoming obsolete, as most of the races humanity met as it moved into space had learned English just as quickly. They were probably more accustomed to dealing with foreign languages—but, on the other hand, Earth has more than her share of languages, so humans had been used to this sort of thing, too, for eons. Of all the planets Archer had heard of, both rumors and confirmed, Earth had by far the widest range of cultures, races, dialects, and languages. Though the Vulcans and others liked to pretend otherwise, Earth was the most cosmopolitan and diverse planet in the charted galaxy.

But diversity didn't suit Archer's purpose at the moment. He needed one narrow thread of talent. It was in that room.

He heard her voice. A charmingly high—"small"—voice, almost a child's voice, but strong and confident at leading the mumble of students through tedious repetitions of alien pronunciation.

"Tighten the back of your tongue," the charming voice suggested.

Then somebody choked.

Oh, it wasn't a choke. Probably alien poetry. Who knew?

Archer was looking forward to having Hoshi Sato's spirit and cheer on his bridge. Good thing, because she would be there about half the time, and most command watches, as the ship's communications officer. The station was a relatively new posting, never before located on the ship's bridge itself, but this was a correction of a problem. The communications officer had turned out to be far more important to the moment-by-moment workings of a ship in space than anyone had expected, even when nobody was talking to anybody. It would be Hoshi's responsibility not only to make sure the crew heard every command, but that all the systems in the ship were communicating with *each other,* from sensors to the red alert klaxons. Hoshi was also in the command line, simply because the com officer always had firsthand knowledge of exactly what was happening.

Then she spotted him lurking in the back of the room. Her youthful face screwed up with concern. The captain never showed up without a reason, and that meant she would be leaving with him. She knew it, he could tell, but he could also see protest rise in her almond eyes. She would try to talk him out of whatever was about to drag her away.

Archer watched her. She was already disappointed, upset, just from seeing him here. Her right eye got a little tighter.

He'd hoped to ease her distress a bit with his Hawaiian shirt, a kind of peace offering, but not much of a disguise. Was it working? Big flowers and uncaptain-like colors, jeans and tennis shoes? About as passive as wardrobe could get. Archer rubbed his hands and tried not to appear as self-conscious as he felt. The shirt he liked, but interrupting a class wasn't so pleasant. He felt like a tardy kid.

"Keep trying," the young lady said to her chanting pupils. She kept her eyes on Archer. "I'll be right back."

As if stepping through a looking glass, she came out of the classroom and skewered him with a pure glare. "You're not here, are you, sir? Not *here.*"

Her voice was musical and happy despite her annoyance. Archer smiled. "Well," he said, "you're here, so I had to come . . . here."

"Outside, please."

Outside was a jungle garden. For all its wildness, it was, in fact, artificial. Everything here was native to Brazil, but had been brought here and nurtured in this domed university under controlled environments. The eerie part was how real it all looked. The only telltale element was the smell. No rot.

"I need you," he stated bluntly as she stepped out before him on the constructed pathway.

"You promised," she moaned. "I took this job because you promised I could finish. There are two more weeks before exams. It's impossible for me to leave now."

Archer managed not to groan at her flimsy excuse. "You've got to have someone who can cover for you." He avoided commenting that it was just a foreign language class and she might have to rearrange her priorities to a more galactic mentality. No, probably not the thing to say right now.

"If there were anyone else who could do what I do," she said, "you wouldn't be so eager to have me on your spaceship."

She had him there.

"Hoshi," he began, but didn't finish quickly enough.

"Captain, I'm sorry. I owe it to these kids."

He almost laughed, though managed to keep from it again. Kids? She was hardly a crone herself. And there were other things at work besides devotion to this particular cluster of students, who would be scattered far and wide in a matter of weeks.

"I could order you," he attempted, just to see what kind of a rise this would get.

"I'm on leave from Starfleet, remember? You'd have to forcibly recall me, which would require a reprimand, which would disqualify me from serving on an active vessel."

He shrugged. "I need someone with your ear."

"And you'll have her. In three weeks."

This angle was all wrong and wouldn't work, Archer knew. She was a sweet and benevolent person, intelligent and clever, but she was lousy at lying, and this was a lie. Nobody was quite this irreplaceable. There were plenty of teachers out there who could gargle in front of a group and get them to repeat it. This wasn't the first time she'd put him off. She was afraid. They both knew she didn't want to go out on an experimental ship on a mission that could turn dangerous on a whim. Hoshi wasn't the pioneer type.

How could he broach the reality? Tell her she was right to hesitate? He wanted to open up and reassure her that being scared of scary things wasn't the same as being a coward.

Except for one thing. She wanted to be out there speaking languages, not down here teaching them, and he knew it. Time for the heavy artillery.

From his breast pocket he took a small device and clicked it on, letting a stranger's voice speak for him—a Klingon voice, speaking the garbled ancient language never heard on Earth before a few days ago.

The tension left Hoshi's brow. Something else replaced it. "What's that?"

"Klingon. Ambassador Soval gave us a sampling of their linguistic database."

"I thought you said the Vulcans were opposed to this!"

"They are. But we agreed to a few compromises."

Hoshi fell silent and listened to the recording gacking and gleching and k'tonking merrily in Archer's hand. Archer kept his lips clamped on any encouragements. He had to give her something worth being scared for. She didn't want to teach—she wanted to *do.* Teachers were always the last to use new information. Hoshi would want to be the first.

Yes, yes?

She was leaning a little closer to his hand. "What do you know about these Klingons?"

"Not much," he tempted. "An empire of warriors with eighty polyguttural dialects constructed on an adaptive syntax—"

"Turn it up."

The Klingon voice got louder. What a language. Sounded like this guy was throwing up.

"Think about it. You'd be the first human to talk to these people," he trolled. He lowered his voice, hunched his shoulders, and leaned toward her. "Do you really want someone else to do it?"

Her eyes flickered like butterflies. She backed off a step, then two, and looked at him without turning again to the speaker in his hand. "Why are you rushing me?" she asked. "What do you *really* want?"

"I want people around me who I already trust," he admitted.

"Because? The mission's so simple . . . deliver a sick man home. Why do you need to trust anybody the way you're saying?"

He shifted on his feet, wobbling into a perfectly

formed fern, and decided that if he could force her to be honest, then he should be, too.

"Because something's wrong."

"Nothing's happened yet," she said. "What could be wrong?"

Archer gazed down at the little device, its alien voice of the unavoidable and complex future.

He clicked it off.

"I don't know yet."

CHAPTER 4

"TRIP, DOESN'T ALL THIS STRIKE YOU AS TOO MANY THINGS going wrong?"

Charlie Tucker frowned at Jonathan Archer's question as the two of them peered out the small ready room's viewport at this side of Spacedock. "What difference does it make what I think? What do *you* think?"

"Don't parry. Just tell me."

"Well, you rushed us into readiness and we're still not ready, but that meant cutting a lot of corners . . . things are bound to tangle some—"

"This much?" Archer settled on the edge of his desk. "Doesn't this strike you as excessive? Something going wrong with almost every shipment of ordnance of any kind? Messages garbled, timelines confused, shipments misdirected—maybe I'm just being overly cautious."

"Paranoid, you mean?"

"I want it to work, Trip."

Tucker smiled briefly. "Well, I think we all want that,

Captain. Although I can't speak for our science officer." He paused, weighing his words. "Since when do we have Vulcan science officers?" he said at last. Tucker's complaint was more of a moan, and there was much more to the statement than he was saying outright. *Vulcans who hadn't earned a place at the top of the team. Rank she hadn't earned, trust she hadn't earned, on a ship she'd never touched, dealing with science her people won't share—a perfect perch from which to keep even more secrets.*

So Archer gave him the bald truth by way of an answer. "Since we needed their starcharts to get to Qo'noS."

Seeming almost in physical pain, Tucker rolled his eyes. "So we get a few maps . . . and they get to put a spy on our ship."

His disdain was justified, to Archer's mind, which made this all the worse. They were selling rank and influence at a pretty low price, on top of the plain risk of a randomly appointed executive officer. Bad judgment, and he couldn't pretend it was anything less.

He looked away from Tucker, out at the bright Spacedock, which would no longer protect them after today. He felt cheapened, as if he'd bent too far backward, and the people feeling the ache were his crew.

"Admiral Forrest says we should think of her as more of a 'chaperone,'" he attempted. Pathetic. Fancy words couldn't massage the gift of authority to someone who didn't deserve it. If anything happened to him, nobody would be taking orders from a "chaperone." The figurehead could very quickly go to supreme power and the crew would be obliged to obey. And he had told Hoshi he only wanted people around whom he trusted. What would he say to her about this?

"I thought the whole point," Tucker rasped, "was to get *away* from the Vulcans."

"Four days there, four days back, then she's gone. In the meantime, we're to extend her every courtesy."

Trip Tucker groaned low in his chest. "I dunno . . . I'd be more comfortable with Porthos on the bridge."

Archer smiled sorrowfully at the idea, and searched for something that might give Tucker a boost. He was interrupted before he began by the door chime. His spine snapped straight. "Here we go . . . come in."

No time to let the red flush go out of his face or the burn out of Tucker's eyes.

There she was, coming in from the bridge on which she didn't really belong. As if to rub in the insult, she was wearing a Vulcan commissar's uniform. Or would it be worse if she were wearing a Starfleet uniform?

She offered Tucker not so much as an elevator glance, and handed a padd to Archer. "This confirms that I was formally transferred to your command at 0800 hours. Reporting for duty."

He took the padd and gave it a cursory once-over, because she expected him to. He took the moment of silence to listen to the steam coming out of Tucker's ears, and hoped it would wane. When he looked up at T'Pol, her nose was wrinkled, her neck stiff, and her eyes shifting back from a brief shot around the room.

"Is there a problem?" he asked.

"No, sir."

"Oh, I forgot." He glanced at Tucker, then over to the couch, where Porthos lay sleeping with three of four paws in the air and his snout off the edge of the cushion. "Vulcan females have a heightened sense of smell . . . I hope Porthos isn't too offensive to you."

He pushed an inflection on the word "females," just enough to prickle her if she could be prickled. The Vulcans were always prancing about how they had heightened this and heightened that, so he winged her with one. His goading seemed to ease Tucker's posture. The engineer relaxed some and took joy in this discomfort for the pretender.

"I've been trained to tolerate offensive situations," T'Pol announced.

Tucker perked up. "I took a shower this morning . . . how 'bout you, Captain?"

T'Pol eyed Tucker, and held her breath as long as she could.

"I'm sorry," Archer began, pausing just long enough for her to think he might be apologizing for stinkiness. "This is Commander Charles Tucker the Third. Sub-Commander T'Pol."

Tucker jabbed his hand out toward her. "Trip. I'm called Trip."

T'Pol took a slight breath. "I'll try to remember that."

Oh, enough. Archer allowed himself an annoyed sigh and plunged into the core of Tucker's very legitimate problem with all this.

"While you may not share our enthusiasm for this mission," he said to T'Pol, "I expect you to follow our rules. What's said in this room and out on that bridge is privileged information. I don't want every word I say being picked apart the next day by Vulcan High Command."

If she happened to be insulted, he declared to himself and silently to Tucker, then her irritation would be due payback for her rudeness. The Vulcans prided themselves on their social decorum, but they were among the most discourteous people Archer had ever met. Truly sophisticated people treated others with more respect just as a matter of course, until given much better reasons otherwise than the Vulcans possessed. Humans had certainly demonstrated that Earth wasn't going backward, wasn't standing still, and wouldn't be impeded by snobbery, so why not help? Like Hoshi, the Vulcans didn't want to take any risks. Unfortunately, they also wanted to act superior about their own reticence.

Archer didn't feel like letting them anymore, and he finally had the influence to make good.

"My reason for being here," T'Pol began, feeling the pressure, "is not espionage. My superiors simply asked me to assist you."

"Your superiors don't think we can flush a toilet without one of you to 'assist' us."

"I didn't request this assignment, Captain," she went on, "and you can be certain that, when this mission's over, I'll be as pleased to leave this ship as you'll be to have me go."

She flinched suddenly. Porthos had moved off the couch and was at her leg, sniffing her knee.

"If there's nothing else . . ." she said stoically.

"Porthos!" Archer scolded—but he had waited five seconds longer than he would've with anyone else on the business end of that soppy nose.

The dog cast him a glance, then moved back to his couch.

"That'll be all," Archer said.

T'Pol seemed for a moment to be unsure whether he was addressing her or the beagle. Good.

Over there, Tucker had sidelined himself, with his arms folded and his shoulder blades pressed against the viewport, and said nothing as T'Pol turned and left the ready room, heading to the bridge, which she now had a legitimate right to occupy.

The door slid shut. The ready room fell to silence, except for the faint whirring of the vents with a gush of fresh air. When Archer turned, Tucker was watching the vent port with an accusatory glower.

"What do you think?" Archer asked.

"I think I ought to lube that fan."

"About *her*, Trip. What do you think about T'Pol?"

"I think she likes us as much as I like her, and welcome to it."

Archer eyed him, Tucker eyed back, and after a moment they both blurted, *"Sir."*

Archer laughed, and was relieved when the engineer finally did, too. They were stuck with the situation, and began here and now to make the best of it. Command didn't mean everything necessarily went Archer's way. This was one of the examples of how the new ship and this whole mission really weren't all his yet. He hadn't proven himself. The ship hadn't. Maybe later both would have the influence to tell offensive interlopers and political hacks to find some gravitons and go fly a kite. That time hadn't come. He made a silent vow to himself and to Tucker that it certainly would.

"You think she's really a spy?" he asked.

"Probably," Tucker said. "If you think she's not going to go back to whoever and tell them how we handled ourselves, then you're more naive than I know."

"No, I'm kinda hoping she does that, actually."

"Me, too. Do I think she's here to steal technology or sabotage the ship or screw us over somehow to botch the mission . . . well . . . no, I don't guess I figure that. Yet."

"It's not enough of a mission to botch," Archer agreed. "We're delivering a guy from here to someplace else. Returning a Klingon national to his home space. It's a gesture of good will, and also to show what we can damned well do on our own, with or without anybody else's favors." He reached down to scratch Porthos on the top of his head, in the little bump where the dog brain was kept, and wished himself the same kind of peace. "The Vulcans may be queasy about helping us, but I honestly don't think they're out to hurt us. I don't think they'd actively wreck our advancement, once we prove we can get there—"

"Maybe you're naive after all," Tucker interrupted. "How many times have you heard them say how we're 'not ready' to go out into the galaxy, or how they're waiting for us to 'prove we're worthy' of the company of others, and all? What if they don't think we're 'worthy' yet and they decide to slow us down some for our own good? I mean, John, I'd be lying if I told you that woman doesn't make me nervous, being here all of a sudden, out of nowhere. Serving as a senior officer! Why would she have to be a senior officer if they just want to keep an eye on us? Don't think there's nothing to that. I'd be peekin' over my shoulder if I was you."

Archer's expression changed. He felt his face grow tense. "Is that a serious recommendation? You think my life could be in danger?"

"With her in that position and the Vulcans thinking we're bad news, hell, yes. Vulcans can be just as devious as anybody, and you'd have to be a sponge to think they couldn't."

Archer nodded charitably. "No, any intelligent being can deceive. It goes with the braincase. Sue me if I'd rather think better of them till proven otherwise."

"Not me. I'll look over your shoulder for you."

"But if we don't give them the benefit of the doubt, then we're doing to them what they do to us, always assuming the worst. I'm not ready to do that yet."

"Guess I'm not as nice as you." Tucker shook his head. "You don't *know* her, John."

Archer sank onto the couch next to his dog, without really relaxing. "No, I don't know her. Not yet." Then a surge of conviction struck him, and his eyes flicked up to meet Tucker's. "But, Trip . . . she doesn't know *me* either."

With a sigh, Tucker indulged in a grim, daring smile. "Not yet."

CHAPTER 5

The Spacedock observation deck was awash with dignitaries, invited guests, officers, ambassadors, mucketymucks, and would-bes. Starfleet brass rubbed elbows with Vulcan emissaries, clusters of pundits, power-grabbers, and publicity wonks, all here on a day's notice. Some showed obvious signs of jet lag and more than a little confusion at the sudden acceleration of launch.

Admiral Forrest was speaking already, even though not everyone was seated yet. They were really hurrying this along.

Jonathan Archer was glad of it. At least they took his determination seriously. He hadn't even called sickbay to make sure the transfer of the Klingon had gone well and the guy was still alive.

He glanced at his sides. Trip Tucker was beside him, and after him was Lieutenant Reed.

On Archer's other side were the newly arrived helmsman, Mayweather, and Hoshi and the Vulcan, T'Pol. He'd feel comfortable but for her presence among people he trusted. Even Mayweather was an associate from two of Archer's previous ships. The only stranger was the Vulcan woman, and she made them all uneasy.

Archer tried to bury his concerns, doubts, and the sniggering insult at having her here with these people who had embraced the faster-than-light program with far more devotion than the Vulcans could muster. He tried to suspend his thousand immediate concerns and do his ceremonial duty—pay attention to Admiral Forrest's bountiful pontifications from the podium.

"When Zephram Cochrane made his legendary warp flight ninety years ago," the admiral was saying, "and drew the attention of our new friends, the Vulcans, we realized that we weren't alone in the galaxy."

The crowd obliged with applause, stretching moments into minutes.

"Today," continued Forrest, "we're about to cross a *new* threshold. For nearly a century, we've waded ankle-deep in the ocean of space. Now it's finally time to swim.

"The warp five engine," the admiral went on, "wouldn't be a reality without men like Dr. Cochrane and Henry Archer, who worked so hard to develop it. So it's only fitting that Henry's son, Jonathan Archer, will command the first starship powered by that engine."

Forrest nodded to Archer. The crowd applauded again as Archer and his command staff stood up and moved away from their seats. Archer kept his eyes from meeting anyone's. The applause should be for Dad and nobody else. Archer knew he was catching the glory by reflection only, and wondered how many other bits of fallout from his father's work had bolstered him in his own climb to command. That couldn't be ignored, and it would be unfair of him to claim otherwise. Bitterness set in again. He would happily have become a shuttle conductor if only Dad had received the honors he deserved and the right to see his ship launched while he was still alive. This was too little, too late.

Damn Vulcans.

He led his crew toward a set of doors while the admiral kept talking.

"Rather than quoting Dr. Cochrane, I think we should listen to his own words from the dedication ceremony for the Warp Five Complex, thirty-two years ago. . . ."

A large screen took over the crowd's attention as it came alive with archival footage of a very elderly Zephram Cochrane, the father of warp drive, giving a speech in front of a throng of scientists, including Henry Archer, a long time ago. Ironically, Archer remembered being present at that speech, before he was even seven years old. Even then he had realized the import of what he was hearing.

"On this site," the crotchety Cochrane began, "a powerful engine will be built. An engine that will someday let us travel a hundred times faster than we can today. . . ."

Archer led his crew through the breezeway to the airlock attached directly to the ship. As they moved, the speech was piped through to the bridge.

The bridge was a compact command center, austere and spartan, mostly steel-walled, with a source of light from hidden panels overhead. There were no carpets or amenities, just various stations with bucket seats, and a maze of gauges, dials, and little scanner screens. In the middle was the captain's chair, to which Archer dutifully moved while the universe watched.

"Imagine it," Cochrane's voice thrummed. "Thousands of inhabited planets at our fingertips . . . And we'll be able to explore those strange new worlds, and seek out new life, new civilizations. . . . This engine will let us go boldly where no man has gone before."

Barely conscious of it, Archer noticed his own lips moving to the words. He stopped and cleared his throat. Everybody was waiting for him now.

"Detach mooring umbilicals and gravitational supports," he ordered. "Retract the airlock and disengage us from the Spacedock. Confirm all break-offs. Internally metered pulse drive, stand by."

"Impulse drive standing by, sir," Mayweather responded. "All sublight motive power systems ready."

At Archer's side, T'Pol appeared. But she didn't repeat any orders, as would a practiced Starfleet officer. She didn't interfere at all. Perhaps she felt as out of place as they thought she was. She took the science station with reserved grace, but seemed out of place and unhappy.

Frozen vapor swarmed through the Spacedock, as if a dragon had breathed across dry ice. Archer leaned forward in the command chair. Around him, the crew was tense and expectant. On the engineering tie-in screen to his left, he saw Trip Tucker standing before the throbbing warp core, looking like an eaglet about to fledge.

In Archer's mind, his father's hand worked the control unit of a model ship, smiling warmly at a little boy who believed in him completely. Every man could do much worse in life than to have a little boy believe completely in him. The father's hand came down, and passed the control unit to a boy's tiny palm. The boy inserted the unit into the model ship.

"Take her out," Archer said finally. "Straight and steady, Mr. Mayweather."

"Ladies and gentlemen," Admiral Forrest's voice overlaid Archer's words. "Starfleet proudly presents to the galaxy . . . the faster-than-light long-range cruiser, *Enterprise!*"

Applause rang and rang in Archer's ears. A shiver went down both arms.

The lean and masculine ship, rugged in construction and blatantly field-ready, undecorated and proud of it, began to move slowly forward, throbbing with power to her innermost bones. Spacedock peeled back from his view and disappeared behind him, like so many memories. Everyone else expected her to be back in eight days, but Archer had other ideas. If the ship stressed out well and he could play his cards right, she wouldn't see a Spacedock for the next six months.

They'd made it. They were out, and with two hours to spare. Now all those dignitaries could go back to bed. Archer forgot them immediately. His eyes were on the forward screen. Open space.

He found his voice again and tapped the chair com. "How're we doing, Trip?"

Behind Trip Tucker's voice, the warp engines pulsed at full power. "Ready when you are," he responded. Sounded both excited and nervous.

"Prepare for warp. Mayweather, lay in a course," Archer said, and glanced at T'Pol. "Plot with the Vulcan starcharts . . . direct course to the planet Qo'noS."

Mayweather's eyes flicked toward T'Pol, but he studiously managed not to look at her. He worked his navigational controls, which only now, as they cleared the solar system, received clearance from the access-classified starcharts brought by their new executive officer.

"Course laid in, sir."

That was it. Never again would the Vulcans be able to hide the location of the Klingon planet from Earth. Sounded like a prime tourist destination, didn't it? Yes, folks, spend your next holiday spitting and howling in the galaxy's newest vacation wonderland!

"Request permission to get underway?" Mayweather looked at Archer.

Archer snapped out of his thoughts. Warp speed . . . high warp. This was it.

He looked at T'Pol and asked silently for confirmation of the course.

She sensed his eyes and looked up. "The coordinates are off by point two degrees."

Mayweather glanced at her, embarrassed and angry. Something about the way she said that . . .

But Archer wasn't about to let her spoil the moment. "Thank you," he said quickly, and waved casually to Mayweather. "Let's go."

"Warp power," Mayweather uttered aloud, though he didn't have to. "Warp factor one . . ."

The ship surged physically. There was a snap of light, and the crescent of Earth was left behind as if by magical invocation. The whole solar system was suddenly no more than a whim.

"Warp one accomplished," Mayweather confirmed.

Archer made eye contact with everyone around him . . . first T'Pol, who had no more criticisms. Then

Reed. He seemed weary, but British propriety kept his shoulders back and tension in check, and he gave Archer a nod of generous encouragement.

Archer smiled, then looked at the little screen with Trip Tucker shepherding his engines. "Trip? You okay?"

"Ready and willing," Tucker responded, but never looked away from the glowing warp core.

"Go to warp factor two."

"Warp two," Mayweather choked.

Another flash, another surge, and the ship shouldered into a multiplicity of speed. Stars blurred. Space itself began to bend to the ship's will.

"Warp two accomplished, sir."

"I like the feeling," Archer offered. "Everybody stable? No jumps in the readings?"

No one spoke up.

"Warp factor three."

Though Mayweather didn't respond, his hands worked on the helm. Another flash. The surge this time was smoother, and in a moment they had made warp three.

"Good," Archer commented. "Everybody take a breath. Check your stations. Hoshi, do a shipwide sweep."

"Shipwide, aye," Hoshi responded, her voice tight. She was terrified. Giving her something to do was sound operational practice. He'd have to make sure she wasn't idle at times like this.

"Let's have warp four, helm."

He barely felt his own voice. Pushing it, yes. He should've cruised at warp two for a day. He didn't feel like waiting. He wanted the first log entry to read immediate high warp.

Somebody gasped, but he wasn't sure who. Probably Hoshi. Couldn't be T'Pol, right? Or Reed.

Not that it mattered. They were all gasping on the inside.

"Respond to me, Travis," Archer steadily insisted.

"Oh . . . yes, sir. Warp factor four, aye. Sorry."

"No problem at all. Doing fine. Feels pretty good, actually. Hear that warp hum? I like that."

His casual conversation seemed to help them all. The power systems whined some at this higher challenge. Lights flashed on several consoles, but nobody called an end to it. Anyone, at any station, could have stopped the progress with an alarm warning. Unless they were at battle stations, even Archer would have a hard time explaining pushing beyond stress once he got a stop warning from one of the crew, almost anywhere on the ship.

No one spoke up. In fact, they were eerily quiet. Hoshi's communications board flickered with green lights from systems deep in the ship's fibrous flanks.

"Warp factor four," Mayweather uttered, "accomplished, Captain. All systems report stable. Helm is steady."

"Trip?"

On the engineering monitor, Tucker finally turned to meet Archer's expectant eyes. "We're all-go down here, Captain. Flow over the dilithium crystals is even. No flux on the power ratios. She looks good."

"Congratulations, Trip . . . everybody. Let's cruise at warp four for a while and see how she does. All hands, standard watch rotation for the next twenty-two hours. T'Pol, how would you like to try the con on for size?"

She looked up, startled. Yes, he'd managed to fluster her. Clearly she hadn't expected to take command at all. She knew she was just some kind of figurehead here and had probably hoped to stay pretty much to what she knew at the science station.

But if the rest of the crew had to endure trials, then so did she. After all, she could've stayed on a nice Vulcan boat if she wanted passivity.

Archer stood up, offering the hot seat.

T'Pol's eyes narrowed. She sensed a trap. Perhaps it was. Under the cloying eyes of the crew, she stood up and moved to the center of the bridge and took the command chair. What choice did she have?

"Good," he said. "Why don't you join me for dinner at change of watch? We can get to know each other. Put the crew at ease, if nothing else."

She eyed him. Just who was suspicious of whom?

"Thank you," she said, not giving anything away.

Choreographing his movements carefully, Archer stepped away from the center and moved to the exit hatchway. The tall, airtight swinging hatch was almost big enough to get through without ducking—almost. He paused before leaving the bridge, turned, and looked at the expanse of space spilling out before the newest Earth ship, named *Enterprise,* as she flashed along on her invisible racetrack.

"We made it, Dad," he murmured. "Couldn't have done it without you."

And in his mind, the model spaceship streaked for the clouds.

CHAPTER 6

VISCOUS PINK FLUID TWISTED IN A JAR. TINY CORKSCREW organisms flitted through the pink like birds in an eternal microsunset. The jar turned, but the liquid and the flitters pretty much stayed the way they were, enjoying their brainless dance.

"Love what you've done with the place. . . ."

Jonathan Archer turned the jar again, watching the little life-forms squiggle.

"Those are immunocytic gel worms," Phlox explained happily. "Try not to shake them."

The quirky alien was in a perfect fantasy here in the ship's minimal sickbay. He had ultimate say over everything. Suddenly he was the senior medical officer on a ship. That didn't happen every day.

Archer paused and watched as the funny fellow arranged, like an old-lady apothecary, dozens of jars, tools, and definitely non-Starfleet-issue medical paraphernalia onto the Plexiglass shelving behind the doctor's computer center. As he handed Phlox the pink jar,

Archer turned his attention to the unconscious Klingon lying on the biobed. He wanted to ask how this fellow was doing. Alive? Almost alive? Would he be able to stand up and walk out of here when they reached Qo'noS?

Or would Archer be forced to hand over a semicorpse to the Klingon reception committee? Not his first choice. He didn't think they'd much like it, either.

He held back the questions. The Klingon was stable, wasn't going anywhere, and he wanted Phlox to feel at ease enough to do a good job. He'd pulled the Doctor out of a secure position at Starfleet Medical, where he had plenty of others making decisions to support him and he had a support system to lean on. Here, even though he didn't seem to know it yet, things would get a lot harder, and fast.

"So, what'd you think of Earth?" Archer asked pointlessly, just to get things rolling.

"Intriguing," Phlox said. Already the word was trite. Aliens always said *intriguing* when they didn't know what else to say. Archer suspected it was being taught at the Customs Center, kind of like bowing in Japan or a lei in Hawaii. "I especially liked the Chinese food. Have you ever tried it?"

Handing off articles from the packing box on top of the desk, Archer shrugged. "I've lived in San Francisco all my life."

Of course, San Francisco had a Chinese restaurant on every third corner, just like any other American city, but he sensed Phlox wanted to have something on him.

"Anatomically, you humans are somewhat simplistic," Phlox said, probably not realizing he was being insulting. "But what you lack biologically, you make up for with your charming optimism. Not to mention your egg drop soup. Be very careful with the blue box."

Gingerly, Archer passed him a funny-looking box with breathing holes punched in both lateral sides. Inside, something skittered that made him almost drop the container. "What's in there?"

"An Altairian marsupial. Their droppings contain the greatest concentration of regenerative enzymes found anywhere."

"Their droppings?"

"If you're going to try to embrace new worlds, you must try to embrace new ideas."

"Ah."

Archer just nodded, annoyed that everybody seemed to be taking classes in etiquette from the Vulcan Institute of Creative Condescension.

"That's why," Phlox went ignorantly on, "the Vulcans initiated the Interspecies Medical Exchange. There's a lot to be learned."

But Archer had stopped paying much attention. Instead, he wandered to the ward and stood over the Klingon. Was he breathing?

"Sorry I had to take you away from your program, but our doctors haven't even heard of a Klingon."

"Please!" Phlox blurted. "No apologies! What better time to study human beings than when they're under pressure? It's a rare opportunity! And your Klingon friend . . . I've never had a chance to examine a living one before!"

"Ensign Mayweather tells me we'll be to Qo'noS in about eighty hours." Archer turned to the intern. "Any chance he'll be conscious by then?"

"There's a chance he'll be conscious within the next ten minutes," Phlox said. "Just not a very good one."

"Eighty hours, Doctor," Archer told him. "If he doesn't walk off this ship on his own two feet, he doesn't stand much of a chance."

"I'll do the best I can." The alien smiled infectiously—and his smile got bigger, bigger . . . bigger . . . weirder . . . "Optimism, Captain!"

Trip Tucker climbed through the ship's cramped crawl space, a laddered passage meant pretty much for maintenance, not really for daily use. Preoccupied with thoughts divided between the ship, the captain, and the Vulcan, he didn't even realize he had company until a boot heel scraped his shoulder. He turned and looked above him.

There, in an open gap between two ladders, Ensign Mayweather was enjoying his off time by squatting on what really was the ceiling. In space, of course, there was no real ceiling, but just an artificial feeling of up and down created by spinning gravitons.

"You're upside down, Ensign," he mentioned.

Travis Mayweather blinked at him. "Yes, sir."

Tucker got the idea he'd interrupted a meditation session or something.

"Care to explain why?" Tucker asked. He really meant *how*.

"When I was a kid, we called it the 'sweet spot.' Every ship's got one."

" 'Sweet spot'?"

"It's usually halfway between the grav-generator and the bow plate." He pointed to a thin conduit crossing below them. "Grab hold of that conduit. Now swing your legs up."

Tucker took a grip on the conduit, but couldn't quite muster the nerve to jump off the ladder, the only stability between him and three decks looming below.

"Swing your legs," Mayweather encouraged.

"Wow . . ." Tucker gulped as an unseen force took hold of him with the slightest encouragement and gave him support as he twirled in sudden zero-G. He still had a grip on the conduit, just in case.

"Now, let go," Mayweather said.

One hand, then the other . . . he laughed at the sensation. Just like basic training! He spun and pirouetted merrily, tucking his legs and stretching them out again.

Then he bumped his head on the ceiling next to where the helmsman sat.

"Takes practice." Mayweather reached for him and helped him find a stable sitting position. "Ever slept in zero-G?"

"Slept?"

"Like being back in the womb."

Tucker paused and eyed him. "Captain tells me you've been to Trillius Prime."

Mayweather nodded. "Took the fourth, fifth, and sixth grades to get there. I've also been to Draylax, and both the Teneebian Moons."

"Mm . . . I've only been to one other inhabited planet besides Earth. Nothing there but dust-dwelling ticks. I've heard the women on Draylax have . . ."

The helmsman nodded drably. "Three. It's true."

"You know that firsthand?"

"Firsthand, secondhand, and thirdhand."

Uh-huh, sailor stories already. Tucker offered a shrug and made no further comment about their slipping back into a pointlessly prepubescent moment. Officers and gentlemen, right?

"Guess growing up a boomer has it advantages," he said, avoiding a comment about how a cow has four. They shared a silly smile.

"The Grand Canyon?"

"No."

"Big Sur Aquarium?"

"Sightseeing was not one of my assignments."

"All work and no play . . . everyone should get out for a little R and R now and then."

"All our recreational needs are provided at the compound."

Well, wasn't this rather like having a dinner conversation with a block of granite.

What was it about Vulcans and common courtesy? Maybe humans should just cut their losses and learn to be stiff and rude.

Little blessings . . . the door chimed and got Archer off the hook of making small talk with a person with whom he should have an awful lot to talk about. He'd known captains and science officers who talked nonstop for the first five watch rotations, just to get to know each other.

Not this time.

"Come in," he said thankfully.

Charlie Tucker strode from the mess hall into the captain's private mess chamber. It was a pleasantly appointed room with a table for four, six if they squished, warmly lit by two candles provided by the captain's steward as a first-meal gift. There was no food yet, but only a basket of breadsticks between the candles. Tucker came all the way in to let the door close and declared, "You should've started without me."

"Sit down," Archer said, afraid he might get away.

Tucker clumped into a chair beside Archer and snatched up a breadstick. Noisily he began to gnaw, paying special attention to the sesame seeds.

T'Pol raised her chin and looked down her nose at him—literally and figuratively—in clear disapproval of the eating habits. Archer smiled. How else *was* there to eat a breadstick except with some noise and breakage? You had to burn a few dilithium crystals to get power, after all.

Archer extended the basket of breadsticks to T'Pol. She obligingly took one and placed it dead center on her plate, then looked at it as if expecting it to explain its intentions.

"T'Pol tells me she's been living at the Vulcan Compound in Sausalito," Archer attempted.

"No kidding," Tucker blurted. "I lived a few blocks from there when I first joined Starfleet. Great parties at the Vulcan Compound."

T'Pol didn't respond, but picked up her knife and fork and began dutifully sawing at the breadstick on her plate. It crumbled almost immediately, and sprayed the tablecloth with crumbs.

"It might be a little easier," Archer suggested, "using your fingers."

"Vulcans don't touch food with their hands."

Where had she made up *that* one? Archer had seen, with his own eyes, Ambassador Soval eating finger food at a reception. Maybe it was a regional thing. Vulcans always talked in generalizations, he was beginning to realize.

"Can't wait to see you tackle the spareribs," Trip Tucker commented as T'Pol changed her approach to the breadstick.

She held it down with the fork, and began to deliberately saw at it with the butter knife, but she glanced forbiddingly at Tucker.

"Don't worry," Archer said. "We know you're a vegetarian."

As if conjured, the steward entered from the galley passage with three plates of food. Two meat, one grilled vegetables. Archer was suddenly glad he'd remembered that little detail at the last minute. Vegetarians on ships had caused complications for ship's cooks for centuries, not to mention allergies and other special needs. Plain baked beans instead of pork 'n' beans. Having aliens aboard would certainly change even more galley plans. T'Pol was all of those.

"Looks delicious," Tucker commented. "Tell the chef I said thanks."

The steward nodded and simply exited.

Archer and Tucker began to eat enthusiastically, but T'Pol ignored her food and continued methodically sawing at the breadstick.

"You humans claim to be enlightened," she said, "yet you still consume the flesh of animals."

Archer caught Tucker's annoyed glance, but got the idea the engineer was enjoying something about this predicament.

"Grandma taught me never to judge a species by their eating habits," Tucker mentioned.

Ah, yes, infinite diversity, Vulcan style.

"'Enlightened' may be too strong a word," Archer pushed on, "but if you'd been on Earth fifty years ago, I think you'd be impressed by what we've gotten done."

"You've yet to embrace either patience or logic," T'Pol accused. "You remain impulsive carnivores."

"Yeah?" Tucker blurted. "How about war? Disease? Hunger? Pretty much wiped 'em out in less than two generations. I wouldn't call that small potatoes."

"It remains to be seen whether humanity will revert to its baser instincts."

"We used to have cannibals on Earth." Tucker leaned closer to her and wagged his eyebrows. "Who knows how far we'll revert? Lucky for you this isn't a long mission."

"Human instinct is pretty strong," Archer supported. "You can't expect us to change overnight."

At this special moment in their relationship, T'Pol succeeded in snapping the breadstick with a rather tidy final cut. She slid the piece onto her fork. "With proper discipline, anything's possible."

She then ate the piece, as if that were really something worth showing off.

Archer managed not to groan. If this turned out to be the only level on which they could converse, then the whole ship was in trouble. Couldn't they be more honest? Talk about important things? Treat each other like intellectual equals instead of zoo animals gaping at each other's quirks over insurmountable gates?

This seemed so unproductive . . . and it really wasn't why he had asked her here, or Tucker either. Wasn't there *some* way to break through to her?

They ate in silence, which seemed to suit T'Pol perfectly well. Apparently Vulcans didn't take meals as social lubrication. This was more like church. It even had the nasty glances from the naughty kid.

Just when Archer thought his head would blow off, Tucker shifted on his seat and asked, "So, Miss TeePol, how long you been on Earth?"

"A few weeks, this occasion. I am not permanently living there."

"Yeah? Where'd you go to school?"

"At which level?"

"Well . . . the latest level."

"I am Ambassador Soval's apprentice in interplanetary sociopolitical studies."

"Really? Got any military training? Like, ever piloted a ship before?"

"Trip," Archer cut off. "She doesn't have to pilot the ship. We have helmsmen for that. She'll get through the next eight days just fine with our support system."

Don't badger. Tucker got the message and fell silent again.

T'Pol finished her vegetables and immediately stood up. "Thank you for inviting me to your meeting. I shall return to my post. I have many studies. I must acquaint myself with the vessel in order to be an effective senior officer."

Archer got to his feet—something he really didn't have to do as commanding officer—and escorted her to the door. "I hope this is only the first," he said graciously. "Thank you for coming, Sub-Commander."

"Yes, Captain. Enjoy your evening."

And she was gone. Archer stared for a moment at the closed door.

"Not bad," Tucker commented, "for an 'impulsive carnivore' such as yourself, Captain."

Archer shook his head in wonderment at all this. "But you notice how forgiving they are of anything the Klingons do, no matter how savage. Humans are unenlightened, but Klingons are 'diverse.' "

"Uppity hypocrites. What a surprise."

"Hey, don't underestimate her. She did, after all, conquer that primitive breadstick with superior discipline."

Tucker laughed.

"Oh, give her some credit," Archer allowed. "At least she knows she's not familiar enough with the ship to be effective yet, and she admitted it. That's not all bad."

"You're bending," Tucker warned. "No bending allowed. Vulcans never bend for us, remember?"

"Are you ready to go to warp four point five?" Archer asked, changing the subject to something they both liked much better than Vulcans.

"Already?" Tucker sat bolt upright. "It's only been—what?—ten hours!"

Archer gave him a sly look and a dangerous grin. "What are we waiting for?"

Tucker seemed to be stricken numb. "I don't know . . . I guess I'm used to bureaucrats and sleepy admirals making the progressive decisions. Twenty memos and a month of means testing, feasibility studies, and role definition."

"We don't define roles here anymore, Trip. We make a list, cut it in thirds, and give everybody a piece. Let's gather the operative minds and take the bridge."

"Delta Watch'll be disappointed."

"They can stay on duty. We're not dismissing them. We're just horning in."

Archer put down his suffering chicken leg. "Come on. I've had it with sitting around being socially unacceptable. Let's do some serious shaking down."

Ten minutes later they were on the bridge, with the primary crew mustered. Malcolm Reed was already on the bridge for some reason. Hoshi showed up a little groggy—she'd been asleep—and Mayweather appeared only a moment after her.

The on-deck bridge crew was uneasy with the appearance of the primary watch, but seemed reassured when all they had to do was stand aside for a few minutes. Any irritation was quickly swallowed in the anticipation of going to warp four point five so many hours early. They could massage their egos later—at higher warp—and enjoy it a lot more.

"Let's all check our readouts," Archer ordered as he took the command chair. "Sing out if you see any irregularities. How have the ratios been?"

"Steady as a stone, sir," Mayweather reported, checking his tie-in to the engineering deck. If anything went wrong down there, he'd be the first to see it on his console, with T'Pol a fast second.

At the science station, she said nothing. Archer could tell, even so, that she disapproved of this early risk.

Well, it wasn't too early for her to have a dose of what made humans tick, other than fresh meat. Archer paused a few moments and listened to the ship. The bleeps and whirrs, the soft hum of warp drive, the twinkle of systems constantly diagnosing themselves. He wanted to memorize those sounds as they were now, doing the right things, feeling the right amounts of energy flow, so he could tell when they didn't sound right.

"Everything seems okay to me," he said, and looked at Mayweather. "Why don't you try four-three?"

Mayweather's shoulders tightened as he worked his helm controls. The sound of the ship made a slight change in pitch—the engines, increasing everything on an incremental level, across the board.

No calls from Tucker . . . so far, so good.

"Warp four point three, sir," Mayweather reported.

They waited and listened. Would something happen?

Or had it just happened, and this was it? This was the sound of success.

"Not much of a change," Reed observed.

"I don't know," Hoshi spoke up. "Does anybody feel that?"

Archer looked at her. "Feel what?"

"Those vibrations . . . like little tremors."

T'Pol cast her a cool glance. "You're imagining it."

Archer thought about what they had said. His science officer neither saw nor felt anything, but his motion-sensor super-ear did.

Of course she did, right? There were bound to be tiny increases in everything. They had just gone from really fast to really-really fast. They had just shortened their trip by several hours, even on the galactic scale. That was a lot of change.

Sure she felt something.

Mayweather was looking at him.

Archer nodded. "Bring us to four-four, Ensign."

This time the ship shuddered, and everybody felt it.

Sounds thrummed from deep places with the new acceleration. Vibrations racked the deck under their feet.

Hoshi grabbed the sides of her seat. "There! What do you call that!"

"The warp reactor is recalibrating," T'Pol explained coldly. "It shouldn't happen again."

But an alarm went off at Reed's tactical station.

Hoshi jumped. "Now what?"

"The deflector's resequencing," Reed told her. "It's perfectly normal."

T'Pol eyed her own board, but said, "Perhaps you'd like to go to your quarters and lie down."

Hoshi cast her a provoked glance. "*Ponfo mirann,*" she said. Vulcan for "butt out"?

Archer watched the women. They were, more or less, a microcosm of the whole crew and all his problems.

"I was instructed," T'Pol responded, "to speak English during this mission. I'd appreciate your respecting that."

Archer interrupted, "It's easy to get a little jumpy when you're traveling at thirty million kilometers a second. Should be old hat in a week's time."

Another alarm tone broke over his words, causing Hoshi to flinch again, but Archer just struck the com panel. "Archer."

"This is Dr. Phlox, Captain. Our patient is regaining consciousness."

"On my way," he said. "Hoshi."

She snatched up her translator padd and joined him eagerly as he headed for the lift. Once the doors had closed and the lift rushed downward into the body of the ship, Hoshi scowled, "I don't like her."

"Why not?" Archer asked.

"Mostly because she doesn't like me."

"Good judgment. You—not her. Besides, I don't think *anybody* likes her much. Of course, she doesn't care whether she's liked. She won't be here that long."

"She wouldn't care anyway."

"You need to relax, Hoshi. This ship is on the cusp of exploration. If you want to speak to aliens and learn new languages, this is the place to be. You'll like it after a while."

"I've just never felt anything like that before. There *were* vibrations that didn't feel right."

"I don't have a doubt of it," Archer offered passively. "The ship's bound to have plenty of instabilities. It'll be our job to track them down, one by one. That's why they call it a 'shakedown.' But you have to do some shaking to get the optimal results."

She sighed and looked like a lost puppy. "Why do all the interesting things have to happen so far from solid ground?"

Archer smiled. Her statement had an ancient ring of truth about it and set his mind to imaginings.

He took her arm gently and squeezed it. "Now, just take things a little slower. Take cues from the people around you instead of the machinery you don't understand."

She looked up at him. "What do you mean by that? What about the people?"

"Most of us have been on ships a lot more than you have. One of the oldest secrets of success on board is to do what the old-timers do. If we sleep, you sleep. If we take a shower, you go take a shower. Eat when we eat. And when things seem scary, take cues from those who've been through scary things before. Stand back and stand by."

"Stand back and stand by," she repeated, tasting the precious advice.

"Right," he said. "In time, you'll be the one the rookies are watching for cues. No matter what the legends say, nobody's born to this."

Though she still appeared doubtful, she did step out of the lift with more confidence. In fact, she led the way to sickbay. Archer took that as a step up.

Even before the door opened to the medical area they could hear the loud growling of the Klingon, like some kind of werewolf on the prowl.

The alien was even more imposing in person than he was just listening in the corridor. Sitting up now, he was absolutely huge. If he stood he would top seven feet. Even sitting he was eye to eye with Archer. Wisely, the doctor had tied him down.

Klaang barked and snapped furiously. *"Pung ghap HoS!"*

Archer flinched at the rage of a strong warrior only inches from him, and was suddenly glad of the security guard, very nearly six-foot-five himself, armed with a plasma rifle and eyeing the delirious Klingon with a hungry glower.

Hoshi was picking and poking at her translator padd, frowning at the information on the tiny screen.

"What's wrong?" Archer asked.

"The translator's not locking onto his dialect. The syntax won't align."

Major faux pas—unaligned syntax.

"DujDaj Hegh!"

"Tell him we're taking him home," Archer said simply.

Hoshi struggled over the words, but she hesitated. The

language seemed, to Archer's ear, to be little more than coughs and hacks.

After a moment, she tried. *"Ingan . . . Hoch . . . juH."*

"Tujpa'qul Dun?"

She frowned. "He wants to know who we are." She didn't add the obvious trailer "I think," even though it was implicit in her tone.

Archer nodded, an equally simple gesture.

Hoshi turned to the Klingon. *"Qu'ghewmey* Enterprise. *PuqloD."*

"Nentay lupHom!"

Hoshi repeated one of the words for her own benefit, then concluded, "Ship. He's asking for his ship back."

Or maybe he was asking to take possession of this one? Archer was reluctant to give him any kind of answer, because neither one would make the Klingon any happier.

"Say it was destroyed."

"SonchIy."

Klaang erupted in a raving protest and roared, *"Vengen Sto'vo'kor Dos!"*

Puzzling over this, Hoshi cocked a hip and screwed up her expression in confusion. "I'm not sure . . . but I think he's saying something about eating the afterlife."

"Try the translator again." Frustrated, Archer tried to contain his impatience.

She worked with the padd. It didn't help.

"I'm going to need to run what we've got through the phonetic processor."

"MajOa blmoHqu!"

Archer turned to her again, but Hoshi could only offer, "He says his wife has grown ugly."

He sighed. If the best translator he knew couldn't do

any better than this, what kind of primitive garble were they dealing with? What he needed was a Klingon who spoke English.

"I'm sorry, Captain," Hoshi said quietly. "I'm doing the best I can."

He was about to give her a word of comfort when Phlox interrupted.

"Excuse me," the doctor butted in as he took a scan of the Klingon. "His prefrontal cortex is hyperstimulated. I doubt he has any idea what he's saying."

"*Hljol OaOqu'nay!*"

"I think the doctor's right," Hoshi said. "Unless 'stinky boots' has something to do with all this."

The ship shuddered under them, sending Hoshi wobbling against the Klingon's bed. She shimmied away and Archer caught her arm and pulled her farther. The guy had spiked leg bands, after all.

"That's the warp reactor again, right?" she asked softly.

"*OaOqu'nay!*"

Archer hurried to the nearest wall com. "Bridge, report on that."

"We've dropped out of warp, sir," T'Pol's voice announced with a shiver of electrical static. "Main power is—"

A burst of static. The com went dead. The lights flickered suddenly—then, consoles all around sickbay began to go dark, one by one!

CHAPTER 7

ARCHER INSTANTLY CROSSED TO THE COM BOOSTER AND played with the controls, but all he could get was a ghost of the action on the bridge.

"T'Pol! Respond!" he attempted. "Tucker! Anybody?"

The com chittered, but there was no sense to it. "It might be the sensors going dark," he muttered, thinking aloud. As he spoke, the sickbay went finally to total darkness. The Klingon raged on his bed. The security guard shambled about, though he didn't know what to do. Archer heard them, sensed them, felt Hoshi's rising fear, but couldn't see a thing.

The com was completely dead. The ship was dark.

In his mind, he saw the action going on all over the ship—crew automatically going to stations, the procedures of emergency and safety snapping into place. He imagined them calling for him on the croaked com system. He felt the ship's power depleting rapidly, felt the drag on his body as speed dropped. Around sickbay,

Phlox's zoo of pet alien organisms chirruped and whistled either in confusion or ecstasy.

"Where are the handheld lights?" he demanded. "Phlox!"

"I don't know, Captain. I haven't inventoried those yet."

"They've got to be in a drawer or a cabinet. Feel around. We can't do anything if we can't see. Hoshi, look around for the beacons. Guard, you, too."

"Aye, sir," the guard rumbled.

Despite her fear, Hoshi started moving. He heard the clap of cabinets and drawers. A few moments later, she was the one who found them.

Instantly, sickbay glowed with red lights. Klaang continued to bellow his maddening protests.

Archer paused and forced himself to think. "Auxiliary power should've kicked in by now . . ." When the Klingon growled and spat again, louder now that nobody was paying attention to him, Archer added, "Do you know how to tell him to shut up?"

More nervous by the second, Hoshi swung to Klaang. "Shut up!" she shouted.

But it didn't work. Diplomacy just wasn't the way today, was it?

"Sedate him if you have to," he snapped to Phlox. "I need to get to the bridge!"

"Captain!"

He whirled at Hoshi's shocked cry. She was moving her beacon across the lateral bulkhead.

Why was she doing that?

Without waiting for him to ask, she hissed, "There's someone in here!"

Archer glanced around the poorly lit room. "Hoshi . . ."

"I'm telling you, there's someone—"

She stopped moving. Archer followed her beacon to the wall again—

A humanoid form!

Like a chameleon, the form had taken on the appearance of the background, complete with certificates and alien life-forms in jars on the shelves! It was barely visible, but now that he focused, there was no mistaking the intrusion.

Once discovered, the creature leaped from its hiding place back into the shadows.

On the biobed, Klaang fell to bizarre quiet. "Suliban!" he growled.

Archer spun, flashing his own beacon across the wall, trying to rediscover the—what was the word? Suliban . . . well, he didn't need any help translating that. Boogeyman.

Another one! Perched high on the wall like a spider! But this one wasn't camouflaged like the other. This one had blotchy skin, almost tie-dyed, with eyes that were clearly evolved for some kind of night vision.

"Crewman!" Archer shouted.

The guard's rifle snapped up just as the Suliban leaped to the ground and met a third one darting from the shadows!

The guard fired. Plasma bullets flashed through the room in quick stroboscopic flashes. Now the action turned to rapid cuts illuminated by the strobes. Klaang yanking around in frustration and shouting in Klingon . . . Hoshi cowering low to avoid the gunfire, scanning erratically with her beacon . . . the guard swinging around to take aim again at something he sensed behind him—

And one of the Suliban leaping onto the big boy. The guard hit the deck, and so did his plasma rifle. The weapon rattled and skidded away.

Archer lunged toward the weapon, hoping he was going in the right direction, but lost his handheld beacon as he struck the deck. Hoshi's beacon was gone now, too. Was she hurt?

The rifle fell into his hands, like a warhorse seeking a rider, and he whirled it toward the nearest Suliban. Taking an instant to be sure he wasn't shooting at his own people, he opened fire.

The Suliban was hit, and flew backward into the wall.

At Archer's right elbow, Klaang stared upward and spat an accusation. Suliban directly overhead! The creature dropped from the ceiling! Archer felt the hard strike of a heavy body on the back of his head and neck. He was driven to the deck under a crushing weight, the plasma rifle trapped under his ribs.

The room went dark again—and very abruptly silent. The silence was scarier than the chaos and rifle shots had been.

Hoshi's little tremor squeaked from under the biobed. "Captain . . . ?"

Archer tried to roll over. This time he felt no resistance. Whatever had been on top of him was now gone. As he got to his knees, a surge of power thrummed up through the skeleton of the ship under his knees and hands. One by one, the consoles began to flicker and light themselves.

Warp power! It was coming back!

Good boy, Trip . . .

The guard was just sitting up, dazed. Phlox rushed to help him. Under the biobed, Hoshi found herself crouched beside the dead Suliban and squirmed suddenly away.

Archer staggered to his feet and looked around as the lights came back on all the way.

The biobed was empty. The Klingon was gone.

And so were the two Suliban interlopers who had survived the past few moments.

Violation. And kidnapping.

Not such a good day after all.

CHAPTER 8

A SHIPWIDE SEARCH HAD TURNED UP NOTHING. THEY weren't onboard. Still, Klaang and the things he called Suliban had gone somewhere, because they weren't here anymore.

Jonathan Archer paced the bridge, agitated. His ship had been breached, the engines temporarily shut down, then just as mysteriously repowered again; intruders had found their way both onto the ship and back off without being tracked. None of that made him feel very good at all.

"We've got state-of-the-art sensors," he complained angrily. "Why in hell didn't we detect them?"

Around him, the bridge crew was virtually sheepish with lack of answers. "Mr. Reed thought he detected something right before we lost power," T'Pol said, as if she really did want to help this time.

Archer whirled on Reed, who was working his tactical and security console. After a moment, the lieutenant offered, "The starboard sensor logs recorded a spatial disturbance."

Trip Tucker leaned over Reed's shoulder. "Looks more like a glitch."

"Those weren't glitches in sickbay," Hoshi noted sharply.

Archer turned to Trip. "I want a complete analysis of that disturbance."

Trip responded by heading for the door, and Archer returned to Reed.

"Where do we stand on weapons?"

"I still have to tune the targeting sensors," Reed admitted unhappily.

"What're you waiting for?" Archer snapped at them.

Reed joined Tucker and hurried off the bridge to do the work that should've been done before they left Earth.

"Captain," T'Pol began, crossing toward him.

He ignored her and swung instead to Hoshi. "The Klingon seemed to know who they were. See if you can translate what he said."

That word . . . *Suliban.* Was it a Klingon word? An accusation or warning? Or was it what Archer thought it was—the name for those creatures?

"Right away," Hoshi said, and also turned to go.

"Captain," T'Pol attempted again.

Finally, with no one else to chew out, order around, or grouse at, he turned to hear what she had to say.

"There's no way you could have anticipated this. I'm sure Ambassador Soval will understand."

"You're the science officer," Archer blurted. "Why don't you help Tucker with that analysis?"

"The astrometric computer in San Francisco will be far more effective."

"We're not going to San Francisco, so make do with what we've got here."

"You've lost the Klingon," she said. Though she sounded reasonable, he still heard that familiar superior attitude in her voice as she finished, "Your mission is over."

He leaned toward her, broiling under the surface. "I didn't 'lose' the Klingon. He was taken. And I'm going to find out who took him."

"How do you plan to do that?" she asked reasonably. "Space is very big, Captain. A shadow on your sensors won't help you find them. This is a foolish mission."

"Come with me."

What he really meant was something along the lines of getting her ass in here, but luckily he still had a little hold on the reins of decorum. He stepped into his ready room and almost instantly whirled on her.

"I'm not interested in what you think about this mission. So take your Vulcan cynicism and bury it along with your repressed emotions."

"Your reaction to this situation," she protested, "is a perfect example of why your species should remain in its own star system."

He closed the small distance between them in an openly hostile manner. Did they have body language where she came from?

"I've been listening to you Vulcans tell us what *not* to do all my life," he fumed. "I watched my father work his ass off while your scientists held back just enough information to keep him from succeeding. He deserved to see that launch. *You* may have life spans of two hundred years. We don't."

T'Pol was affected by his words, perhaps more by his passion, but she didn't back down.

"You *are* going to be contacting Starfleet," she said, "to advise them of the situation."

"No, I'm not," he said with a warning glower. He hoped his message was clear, because clarifying further wouldn't be either polite or pretty. "And neither are you. Now get the hell out of here and make yourself useful."

With nothing more to say, she had no choice but to simply leave. He couldn't imagine Reed or Tucker welcoming her help or even her presence in their work. That was her problem, something she had set up for herself with her own lack of manners.

Archer stalked the ready room—which wasn't much of a stalking space at all, but only a tiny excuse for an office where the captain might be able to be alone once in a while. He didn't really like it here, but was determined to get used to it. The space came in handy just now, as a good place to chew out the sliver under his fingernail—namely, T'Pol.

Bitter and impatient, he struck the com on his desk. "Sickbay, Archer. Phlox, I'm coming down there and I want some answers ready when I arrive. Make them up if you have to, but give me something."

Sickbay never responded. He never gave Phlox the chance.

Within moments he was stalking the corridors instead of his ready room, thumping down through the tubes and access ways directly to the sickbay deck. It wasn't exactly faster than the turbolift, but at least he wasn't standing still while the box rushed him around the ship. He didn't lose many seconds, and he managed to use up enough frustration that, by the time he plunged through the doors into sickbay, he was ready to listen.

Dimly lit except for the surgical lamp shining down on the dead intruder, sickbay was almost like it had been during those terrible moments of attack. Phlox's gloved hands were busy inside the opened chest of the dead creature. He picked enthusiastically through the entrails as Archer watched, unmoved.

"Mr. Klaang was right about one thing," the doctor said. "He's a Suliban. But unless I'm mistaken, he's not an ordinary one."

Archer's throat tightened. How could he tell that this Suliban was special if he had no experience with what an ordinary Suliban was? And he didn't feel much like taking biology lessons. Were there short answers?

"Meaning?"

"His DNA is Suliban . . . but his anatomy has been altered. Look at this lung. Five bronchial tubes. It should only have three. And look at the alveoli clusters. They've been modified to process different kinds of atmospheres."

"Are you saying he's some kind of a mutant?" Archer asked, going for those short answers as deliberately as possible without discouraging information he might need.

"Yes, I suppose I am. But this was no accident, no freak of nature. This man was the recipient of some very sophisticated genetic engineering."

Like a kid in a candy store, Phlox almost giggled with delight at his discovery. He activated a tiny instrument with a thin red beam and shined the light on the Suliban's dappled face.

"Watch this."

He moved the light, revealing that the skin had changed color, perfectly matching the hue and intensity of the red light.

"Subcutaneous pigment sacs."

He tapped a control on the little instrument and the

color of the light changed to blue. He shined it on the Suliban's clothing this time, instead of its face. The clothing also adapted to the new color. The clothing?

"A biomimetic garment!" Phlox piped, delighted.

Archer didn't even bother trying to control his amazement. The skin he could understand. How did these people make their clothing biological enough to do the same thing?

"The eyes are my favorite," Phlox went on. He lifted an eyelid on the corpse, exposing a superdilated pupil that glowed nearly phosphorescent. "Compound retinas. He most likely saw things even your sensors couldn't detect."

Like my sheer anger? Archer thought. Even a dead guy should be able to pick that up.

"It's not in their genome?" he asked.

"Certainly not. The Suliban are no more evolved than humans. Very impressive work, though . . . I've never seen anything quite like it."

No more evolved than humans. Yeah, we're still practically microbes compared to all you demigods out there.

Determined to raise the veil of ignorance even if he had to kick somebody out of the way, he asked, "What do you know about them? Where do they come from?"

"They're nomadic, I believe," Phlox said, apparently not catching the fact that his captain was about to reach down his throat and pull the information out physically if it didn't start coming faster and more voluntarily. "No homeworld. I examined two of them years ago. A husband and wife. Very cordial."

The word stuck in Archer's craw. He couldn't imagine cordiality at this particular moment, from the Suliban, from himself, or anyone else. He didn't even want any.

"Look, Doctor," he began tersely, "I'm not in a pleasant mood. I don't want to hear about anything nice or cordial or even intriguing right now. I want to know where the Klingon went, how the Suliban got onto this ship, and how they got off it. Something tells me they didn't jump out a space hatch and go for a random free-float. They went some*place*. I mean to find out where. None of the answers to those questions is bound to be nice, so you don't have to feel obliged to smile or twinkle at me anymore." He jabbed a finger at the body on the bed. "You have the only piece of concrete evidence we own. I'm giving you my permission to get ugly. If you have to set up candles and a Ouija board and bring this corpse back to life, I want to know how they did what they did today on my ship. Do I have to say any of that a second time? Good."

Trip Tucker had the distinct displeasure of working side by side with the Vulcan female at the sensor data station in main engineering. Still, it gave him a chance to see what she knew, just how much of a token she was in practice. That Vulcans had a strong science base in their education and also their natural predilections couldn't be denied. Hiding a spy as a science officer became the convenient and most obvious trick. There was too much about this woman that was just plain obvious.

Working made Tucker feel better. No matter what they did, he hadn't been able to find any systems failure or falloff. The intruders had flickered the power flow just enough to do what they wanted to do—steal the Klingon—then let everything come back without damage. No damage at all.

Why would they go to all the trouble of figuring out the technology, the security system, sneaking aboard, hiding themselves, shutting down the power, finding a prisoner, stealing him, and sneaking back off the ship, and go to the extra bother of *not* hurting or breaking anything? You'd have to work at that.

"How about this?" he pointed at the newest flush of data on the sensors.

"It's just background noise," the Vulcan's monotone voice stated. "Your sensors aren't capable of isolating plasma decay."

"How can you be so damned sure what our sensors can do?"

"Vulcan children play with toys that are more sophisticated."

Tucker stopped what he was doing and took a moment to reflect on this, which was just a plain fake-out. She knew better, and worse—she knew *he* knew better. Either she was playing, or enjoying another insult.

"Y'know," he began, fed up, "some people say you Vulcans do nothing but patronize us, but if they were here now . . . if they could see how far you're bending over backward to help me . . . they'd eat their words."

Her dark eyes barely registered that he had said anything at all. "Your captain's mission was to return the Klingon to his people. He no longer has the Klingon."

"I realize he's only a simple Earthling," Tucker responded acridly, "but did it ever occur to you that he might know what he's doing?"

She was silent. Of course, he'd put her in a bad position. Even impolite Vulcans knew better than to openly criticize a commanding officer's decision before that decision had played out. At least not too much.

Tucker laid off the snide tone and tried something

else. "It's no secret Starfleet hasn't been around too long . . . God knows you remind us of it every chance you get, but does that mean the man who's been put in charge of this mission doesn't deserve our support?" He waited a moment to see if his words got a rise out of her. "Then again," he added resentfully, "loyalty's an emotion, isn't it?"

She looked at him, and he could tell a response was forming—what would she say? Under that stony facade and the gloss of having a "mission" of her own, what did she really think of Jonathan Archer? He knew, of course, what she'd been told, probably all her life, about humans and Starfleet and Earth culture, because she parroted it mightily. Still, anybody or any race who didn't embrace something new—new people and relationships—would eventually just sit down and finish dying.

Before she could say anything, though, Captain Archer stalked in, obviously annoyed and impatient.

Who could blame him?

"Any luck?" he demanded.

Tucker glanced at the Vulcan. "Not really."

T'Pol had a longer version. "My analysis of the spatial disturbance Mr. Reed saw indicates a stealth vessel with a tricyclic plasma drive."

"If we can figure out the decay rate of their plasma," Tucker said, "we'll be able to find their warp trail."

"Unfortunately your sensors weren't designed to measure plasma decay."

Both men looked at her with varying degrees of resentment. She didn't mean the "unfortunately" part.

Tucker didn't make any comment. But the new communications officer walked in behind Archer and stopped short, looked around engineering at the massive pulsing warp core and the overwhelming complexity of consoles and scanners. Apprehension showed in her eyes.

She sidled toward them on the farthest side of the deck. "Are you sure it's safe to stand so close to that?" Her tone was half-joking, but only half.

"What've you got?" Archer asked sharply.

"I've managed to translate most of what Klaang said. But none of it makes any sense." She handed him a padd.

The captain took it and read the screen. "Nothing about the Suliban?"

"Nope."

Archer now turned to T'Pol and skewered her with a glare. "That name ring a bell to you?"

"They're a somewhat primitive species from Sector 3641. But they've never posed a threat."

"Well, they have now."

Tucker snickered at her. Yet another "primitive" species for the Vulcans to chide? Did she think of the Suliban the way she thought about humans? If so, were they more capable of subterfuge than she gave them credit for?

"Did he say anything about Earth?" Archer asked Hoshi.

She shrugged. "The word's not even in their database."

Archer eyed the padd again. Tucker watched him, and wished he could help.

"It's all there," Hoshi said weakly. "There were only four words I couldn't translate . . . probably just proper nouns." She wanted to help, too, but Archer's problem wasn't improving.

The captain strode away a few steps, contemplating

what he saw on the screen."Jelik . . . Sarin . . . Rigel . . . Tholia . . . Anything sound familiar?"

T'Pol hesitated, uneasy. Seemed her goals were at cross-purposes. Or worse, maybe they weren't.

"T'Pol?" Archer sternly pressed.

She paused again, glanced at Tucker, who was careful to give her one of those get-cracking looks.

"Rigel," she finally began, "is a planetary system approximately fifteen light-years from our present position."

Tucker watched and held his breath. Of course, Earth had known about the blue giant Rigel for generations, and other stars like Altair and Arcturus, but this was the first he'd heard of settled planets there.

"Why the hesitation?" Archer challenged.

Tucker almost blurted *ah-hah!*—but he held back. Archer looked as if he might be ready to pull this gal's eyebrows off if she didn't give, and quick.

Realizing she was about to knock the stick off his shoulder again, she decided to shell out.

"According to the navigational logs salvaged from Klaang's ship, Rigel Ten was the last place he stopped before crashing on your planet."

Though Archer's face flushed with new anger, he plainly wasn't surprised. "Why do I get the feeling you weren't going to share that little piece of information?"

"I wasn't authorized to reveal the details of our findings."

There it was—the problem in a nutshell. "Our" and "your"—"we" and "they." She was here, but she wasn't yet on the team.

Tension mounted. Archer shared a pointed glance at both Tucker and Hoshi. Tucker held his own expression in careful check, not knowing which side of this teeter-totter would be the best one to be on. Should he fan Archer's anger and therefore his strength of will, or should he mollify the situation and hunker down for more efficiency?

Better not choose right now. The captain would signal soon enough which direction he wanted to go.

Controlling himself valiantly, Archer was scarier now than if he'd been yelling. He glowered at her like a cat.

"The next time I learn you're withholding something," he warned, "you're going to spend the rest of this voyage confined to some *very* cramped quarters. Understood?"

T'Pol's expression was hard to read, but she didn't have any snotty remarks. In fact she said nothing at all.

Archer hit the wall com. "Archer to helm."

"Aye, sir," Mayweather responded from the bridge.

"Go into the Vulcan starcharts and find a system called Rigel. Then set a course for the tenth planet."

"Aye, Captain, right away."

Turning to T'Pol, Archer strictly said, "You're going to be working *with* us from now on."

She paled a little, but owned up to her reasons. "I'm sorry you feel slighted. But I agree with Ambassador Soval's restraint in giving Earth too much information. Perhaps the last thing we need is another volatile race in space with warp power. You may easily go out and get yourselves killed. It may be a mistake to have helped you so much, to give you so much before you are ready."

"So *much?*" Archer barked. "You'd better use the next portion of your long lifetime to go back over the records and see just how much we've done on our own, in spite of your cultural cowardice."

"Cowardice?" Her eyes widened.

Over to the side, Tucker smirked and pressed his lips flat with delight.

Archer closed the step between him and her. "I've been thinking about Vulcans all my life. You've been in space a long time, and suddenly the game is complex. Vulcans are logical, but it won't be enough. You've been advanced for a thousand years, and suddenly you're being overrun by us rabbits. The clock is ticking. All sorts of species are moving out into the galaxy. Maybe you don't need another volatile race out there, but guess what—they're everywhere. The galaxy will be driven by passion, not prudence. You haven't been holding back because you think we're so primitive—if you thought that, you wouldn't be bothering with humanity at all. Being logical allows you to say, 'That is a new idea; therefore it hasn't been proven; therefore I don't have to pay any attention to it.' "

"Shall we give you the knowledge to rush out into the galaxy and cause chaos?" she gulped. "Humans claim some right to know that which has been earned by others—"

"We never said that. You offered. On the galactic scale, thirty years this way or that is nothing. When you see somebody is ready to walk, why hold back? There's more going on with you people."

He narrowed his eyes and unplugged the floodgate he'd been saving for Soval all these years.

"You're not the cutting edge anymore, are you?" he badgered. "In a thousand years, why has Vulcan progress been so slow? And here comes Earth, making wild advances in less than two hundred years. You're dragging behind, and now you need us more than we need you. Why else would you want to come and teach the apes how to sew? I think all this is happening because you're plain scared of being out there alone anymore."

Stunned, T'Pol parted her lips again. Nothing came out this time. She never blinked, as if staring at a flashing billboard declaring his words to the known galaxy. He was saying the Vulcans were doomed. Nobody had the guts to say that to their faces.

Archer backed off now, but pointed at her with a determined finger. "You get on that warp trail. And you'd better find something or be able to explain why not in *very* clear terms. Dismissed."

T'Pol blinked almost as if he'd slapped her. She turned on her heel and exited without a word, taking a cloud of confusion along on her shoulders.

Hoshi squirmed a little and said, "I'll . . . I'll keep learning Klingon."

"Good idea."

He handed her the padd.

When Archer and Tucker were alone in the steadily pulsing warp chamber, the captain finally allowed himself a moment of quiet contemplation. He flexed his shoulders, took a deep breath, and let his arms sag. He really wanted to talk to his father.

Instead, there was Trip Tucker, offering him a sympathetic and curious gaze.

"Maybe now we know why we had so many quirks and misdirections with the last three days before launch," Archer contemplated. He turned to lean on the console that had provided such little information.

"You think they infiltrated before we left Earth?" Tucker said.

Archer shrugged. "I don't know. It's a possibility.

Getting off the ship is far less problematic than getting on, but where they went presents us with a goading mystery. I don't like goading mysteries."

"Yes, you do," Tucker drawled. "They had a ship following us, and they went over there."

"If we can find the trail, we'll follow them. If not, I'll go to Qo'noS anyway and start there. Klaang's mother might know something."

Tucker shook his head in worried respect for the sheer gall of that plan. "Why would these Sulibans want to blow our chances to make nice with the Klingons?"

"Might not be it at all. For all we know they might have a personal grudge against Klaang."

"Or . . . maybe they want to ruin our chances to make nice with the Klingons, John."

Archer smiled cannily to reassure him. "I'm not missing that one, Trip, believe me."

Tucker shifted on his feet. "You were pretty hard on Lady Jane. You never had your own pet Vulcan to kick around before, did you?"

"No, and I mean to be harder on her. She's about to discover what the term 'short leash' means."

Appreciatively Tucker nodded and bobbed his brows. "Probably smart, now we know for sure she's been hiding information from us on purpose."

"She'd better knock it off, too." Abruptly, Archer turned grim. "She's my science officer now, not Soval's patsy. She'll learn that lesson over the next week if I have to tattoo it on her tongue."

"Good thing it was you chewing her out instead of me. I'd have punched her in the nose."

"She'd hit me back," Archer said. "And she'd probably break my jaw."

Tucker grinned, though rather drably. "She, uh . . . she came on the ship about the same time as all our little troubles started . . ." He broached the subject, then let it hang there. He didn't seem to have quite the conviction for a direct accusation.

Archer accepted what the engineer was saying. The idea wasn't new to him. He'd be silly to ignore it. "We'll wait and see. Vulcans are reserved. They don't converse. She's just learning about us. As Vulcans go, she's very young. I get the feeling she's as much in the middle as we are. She could be just echoing what she's been taught all her life, and doing what she was told to do. Just a feeling, though." Archer offered him another smile, a little different from the one before. "Anyway, I won't ignore your concerns. In the meantime, you organize a landing party. Make T'Pol part of it."

"Do I have to?"

"It'll show her which team she's on. And Hoshi and Reed. And Mayweather's spent his whole life in space dealing with merchants and travelers. Let's use what we have and get this done."

CHAPTER 9

HUMANS WERE GETTING HELP FROM THEIR VERSION OF "future" people—the Vulcans—who had advanced technology to give. Was it so unwise for Silik's people also to have assistance?

Yet he was troubled and made to feel small by the future beings. Like strangers on the shore, they gave gifts without reasons, asked for trust without substance. Why? If only to play for affection, everyone gave gifts for reasons. Certainly these people had no need of Suliban affection.

Silik stood before the Klingon, Klaang, who was constrained in a medical chair, sitting upright, monitored by the two Suliban physicians. Tubes and devices of bizarre natures were hooked into the Klingon's body. He was bathed in the blue glow of the temperature light, and lolled with the groggy results of having been thoroughly drugged.

"Where is it?" Silik persisted in the Klingon's native language. He had asked the question three times before.

"I don't know." Klaang responded for the fourth time.

"We're not going to harm you. Tell me where it is!"

"I don't know."

Frustrated, Silik looked at the physicians. "Are you certain he's telling the truth?"

"Absolutely certain," one of them answered, and he seemed to believe it.

Silik bent forward toward Klaang. "Did you leave it on your ship? Did you hide it somewhere? Is it on *Enterprise?*"

Klaang's enormous head rolled to one side. "I don't know what you're looking for."

As he realized this line of questioning had solidified and would offer no progress, Silik thought about different approaches that might shake the Klingon's mind.

After contemplating for a moment, he attempted, "What were you doing on Rigel Ten?"

"I was sent to meet someone."

"Who?"

"A Suliban . . . female . . . named Sarin."

At last—the first bit of useful information.

"And what did Sarin give you?"

"Nothing."

But Silik now had a tidbit upon which the day might turn. From a single name, he had an idea of where to begin.

He turned away from the Klingon and to the physicians charged, "Keep him alive while I'm gone!"

Enterprise
Shuttle deck

"Once we've tied down, we'll be descending into the trade complex. It's got thirty-six levels."

Archer paused and looked at T'Pol, indicating that she should take over. The crew should become accustomed to hers as the voice of the science officer.

"Your translators have been programmed for Rigelian. However, you'll encounter numerous other species. Many of them are known to be impatient with newcomers. None of them have seen a human before. You have a tendency to be gregarious. I suggest you restrain that tendency."

"You forgot to warn us about the drinking water," Tucker complained as he belted his jacket and took one of the communicator/translator devices she was handing out to the landing party.

Archer didn't make any comments. If she was going to keep sniping at them with sentences like that, then she deserved what she got back. Beside him, Tucker, Reed, Mayweather, and Hoshi Sato were veritably twitching with anticipation. A new planet! Strange new worlds.

T'Pol didn't even get Tucker's comment. She went on to the next thing. "Dr. Phlox isn't concerned with food and water. But he does caution against intimate contact."

Archer glossed over that one, disliking the idea of treating his command staff like cadets on leave. "The Vulcans told us Klaang was a courier. If he was here to get something, then whoever gave it to him might know why he was taken. That was only a few days ago," he added optimistically, "and a seven-foot Klingon doesn't go unnoticed. T'Pol's been here before, so follow her lead."

He gave her a glance of what he hoped was confidence.

"Where do we rendezvous if we find something?" Hoshi asked.

"Back at the shuttlepod. And no one goes anywhere alone. From what I've heard about this place, it's an alien version of an Oriental bazaar. Don't stop to buy trinkets. Ask simple questions, get direct answers. If you don't like what you hear, move on. There are a lot of people down there, or versions of people. Don't get swallowed up. Watch each other. Clear?"

Whether it was or not, they were on their way. The six-seat subwarp shuttlepod was functional, but not really comfortable, and the trip down to the planet seemed longer than it was.

Mayweather brought the pod into the atmosphere and found himself bucking snow-torn slopes and high winds.

"Approaching what appears to be a landing deck." He squinted out the windshield. "I see a trail of lights. Runway, possibly."

"I'd say this spaceport accommodates all kinds of craft," Archer confirmed, just to make them all feel better. They might be strangers here, but they were coming to a place that was used to strangers. Coming into a cosmopolitan spaceport would be much easier to tolerate than invading a tribal clutch or a village.

In fact, when they finally found the landing pad in the whipping veils of snow, their shuttle turned out to be the smallest thing around, in a swarm of dozens of ships coming and going at the same time. The sight was eerily familiar to anyone who recognized a travel center. Something about it was reassuring to Archer, as they approached and were received as a matter of course. No fanfare, no ceremony, no warnings or threats.

Beacons and trails of blue and yellow landing lights branched out in patterns both distinguishable and not, at least enough to get them down safely. T'Pol used her knowledge of this place to secure a parking spot where the shuttlepod had a chance of not being plundered, and they immediately disembarked and broke into teams.

Trying to appear casual, Archer went first to the dock-master's control tower. After all, something had to come and go from here with Klaang aboard. He certainly hadn't popped in out of thin air, so there had to be a trail.

He and Hoshi were ushered through a tubular construction with lots of bridges into a central control area with windows on every side, couched by banks of controls and broken every few seconds by the sweep of a beacon from the runways. The dockmaster himself was a huge burly alien preoccupied with traffic.

"Pardon us," Archer began, hoping the translator didn't get it wrong. "I'm Captain Jonathan Archer of Starfleet."

"Who? What planet is that?"

"It's not a planet. It's an organization. The planet is Earth."

"Good for you. The visitor's center is on Quintash Plaza."

"Thanks very much. Before we go, would you answer a few questions for us?"

"There's a manual on the wall in the corridor. Read it," the alien rumbled. "Next time, approach from the mountains. Less crosswind."

"Thank you again . . . I'd like to know whether a Klingon vessel of any kind came through here about five or six of your days ago."

"Five or six days? Do you realize how much traffic we process in a single day?"

"You must keep records," Archer suggested, glancing at Hoshi. "This was a one-man Klingon scoutship."

"What species are you?"

"Human. We're called humans."

As if congratulating him, an alarm went off and lights flashed on the dockmaster's console. The dockmaster hammered on what might have been a keyboard, then checked a monitor.

"Elkan nine, raise your approach vector by point two radiants!"

When the alarm stopped, the dockmaster hammered something new into the keyboard and the monitor changed.

"It was *seven* days ago. A *K'toch*-class vessel."

"Does it say who he was here to see?" Although the question was probably out of line or classified, Archer took his best shot at getting what he wanted.

"What it says is that he arrived at docking port six and was given a level one biohazard clearance."

Archer kept from clapping his hands—he would never have given up information like that just for the asking! At least this guy had no such guardrails. "You don't seem very interested in what people do here."

"Our visitors value their privacy," the dockmaster said, even though he had just handed over information Klaang probably never wanted known. "It wouldn't be very *tusoropko tuproya plo* business they're in."

Archer flinched at the sudden change in sounds and looked at Hoshi, who busily adjusted the communicator/translator.

"It's all right," she said. "Rigelian uses a pronominal base. The translator's just reprocessing the syntax."

Who cared? Archer avoided telling her nobody was interested in how it did what it was doing, as long as it succeeded and he could keep talking to this person.

"Do you have any records of a Suliban vessel coming in around the same time?"

"Suliban? I don't know that word. Your device must still be malfunctioning."

The dockmaster went back to his work, turning his idea of a shoulder to the newcomers. If the body language of a mollusk was anything Archer could trust, he got the idea the alien was all done talking. Had he asked the wrong question? Or the exactly right one?

He motioned to Hoshi, muttered another useless thank you, just in case he needed it later, and led the way out into the corridor.

"He's lying," she told him immediately.

"I know. But he has no reason to tell us anything. He's probably more scared of whoever wants him to keep silent."

"Why would he be?"

"You saw the Klingons and the Suliban. They're both a little more rugged than you and I appear to be. Whose threat would you take more seriously?"

"Then we still don't know anything."

"We know for certain that Klaang was here."

"We knew that before, didn't we?"

"Yes," Archer agreed. "But now, if I read my dockmasters correctly, somebody else will know we're here looking for him. Let's go down to the Plaza and appear obvious, shall we?"

The main downtown area was an ancient, towering, weatherworn complex that seemed to have been constructed over several decades. Architectural styles ran the gamut here, as did the age of the buildings. In some cases, new structures were built right on top of old ones, without bothering to demolish. The city was swirled on the outer reaches with inhospitable subarctic terrain and constant winds and snows. Plumes of steam blasted constantly from geothermal vents that kept the buildings from freezing.

Within the city itself, things were about twenty degrees warmer than the spaceport complex, just from the tightly clustered buildings and narrow streets, which didn't allow the arctic blasts to dominate. Haze hung in the air, perforated by shafts of artificial light. Myriad species went about their private business, moving in and out of concealed and sometimes locked trading alcoves. Some were in uniform, others in indistinct robes or layered with jewelry. Many carried weapons.

The flavor of the old West was palpable.

"This place reminds me of somewhere," Archer commented, glancing at a mammoth carpet-haired beast of burden with legs like tree stumps and the smell of a pig farm. "If it were a desert, I'd swear I've been here before."

"And I'd worry about your taste in vacation spots," Hoshi murmured, flinching from a slimy individual who passed by on their left.

Alien insects came to investigate them—large insects the size of birds on Earth. They hovered, and one perched on Hoshi's head for a moment, but became quickly disinterested.

"They don't seem harmful," Archer shored her up.

Hoshi shivered. "Jellyfish don't *seem* harmful either. But don't stick your hand under one."

"Look—this must be the Plaza." He led the way to a vast, cavernous thoroughfare of bridgelike walkways that crisscrossed each other well into the sky and for miles in three directions from where they stood. The concourse was poorly lit, just enough to walk by. As Archer looked out over the incredible complex, he began to worry for his other crewmen. This wasn't the kind of place anyone wanted for a first venture into the galactic wilds.

"Shouldn't we call the captain?"

Travis Mayweather's question was fraught with doubts and misgivings. Quite normal.

Malcolm Reed, on the other hand, blithely followed their alien contact into the trade complex, climbing to the fifth level with a quiver of excitement in his stomach. Around them chattered a cacophony of strange sounds and a sea of deep-green lighting.

"Maybe we should wait," he said to the ensign.

Mayweather hunched his shoulders and called to their very odd guide. "How much longer?"

"It's not very far," the alien called over his—was that a shoulder? "I promise you."

"Are you sure his name was Klaang?" Reed asked again. "Couldn't it have been another Klingon you saw?"

"It was Klaang. I'm certain. I'll show you exactly where he was."

The alien's confidence was encouraging. His unwillingness to describe where he was going, however, was not, and Reed had his doubts. They kept moving.

"I think somebody's following us," Mayweather said, glancing behind them.

"Nonsense. You're just uneasy."

"Then why are the shadows moving in my periphery?"

"They're alien shadows. They probably have arms as well."

"Funny, sir."

"Of course."

"Look at that!" Mayweather pointed ahead of them as the lights changed—literally—to red.

Alien music pervaded the air just above the comfort range for conversation. In an archway off to one side, two mostly undressed alien women squirmed and writhed to an unusual rhythm. It almost sounded Eastern European, but Reed dismissed that as coincidental. Between the women was a thin lantern with dozens of butterfly-type creatures flitting around the light.

As he and Mayweather watched, rapt by the sight, the women squirmed closer to the lantern. One of them tipped back her head and emitted an eight-inch tongue that snared one of the butterflies.

An instant later, the second woman did the same. Were they competing?

Only now did Reed and Mayweather realize they had been joined by a gathering of other spectators to watch the butterfly dance. The crowd seemed to run the course from arousal to disgust. Rather familiar, at the moment, Reed noted.

Ah, yes, a brothel. What a shock. If he had been sketching out the most stereotypical mecca in all literature, this would be at its center. Didn't anyone do anything subtle anymore?

"Would you like to meet them?" the alien man offered, waving a large narrow paw at the women. "I can arrange it."

Mayweather grimaced. "Was this where you saw Klaang?" he persisted.

"No, no, not here. I'll show you where. But first, you should enjoy yourselves! Which one would you prefer?"

"We're here to learn about the Klingon," Reed reiterated, though he found himself watching the women and the . . . "Are those real butterflies or some kind of hologram?"

Mayweather took his arm. "We should get going, sir."

"Yes . . . absolutely. You're right."

They moved down the tubelike arcade of erotic dalliances from topless fire-eaters to costumed performers of every stripe. Reed slipped in front of the alien man who was supposed to be guiding them and began to ignore the fellow's gestures of this way or that. Obviously he was more of a tour guide than an informant.

"Gentlemen, gentlemen!" the alien called, suddenly desperate. "Perhaps you'd prefer to watch the interspecies performance?"

"You don't know anything about Klaang, do you?" Mayweather bluntly accused.

"Of course I do, but there's no reason to hurry, is there?"

"Interspecies performance?" Reed asked.

"Lieutenant," Mayweather called wearily, "this man has no intention of helping us."

Reed nodded. "Perhaps another time."

Disappointed, their guide sagged in several places and disappeared into the crowd. Reed and Mayweather moved in a completely different direction, just in case the fellow held a grudge.

"I can't believe we fell for that."

Reed stifled a groan and avoided mentioning that he couldn't believe it either, and he didn't want to tell this story. Perhaps he could make something up that would be more interesting to hear about and less trite in the telling.

He shrugged. "We *are* explorers."

Trip Tucker had gotten himself paired off with T'Pol. Not the most natural of buddy systems, but he wanted to keep an eye on her. If she had a chance at subterfuge, this would be the place.

She was over there, speaking to a uniformed alien—maybe a security hireling or this place's version of a constable. He looked just as seedy as everybody else here. Tucker felt like maybe he should've let himself get five o'clock shadow before he came.

He didn't like it here. It was dirty and unfriendly. Nobody trusted anybody. Nobody deserved trust. Too many people, too little square dealing.

All he could do was wait. They had agreed on a game plan. She would do the talking and he would do the watching.

He was sitting among a weird assortment of beings, waiting, and hating every minute of it. The place was smoky, smelly, and dim. He'd never see a knife coming at him.

And over there was this alien infant, screaming its tentacles off. He couldn't help but keep looking at it. Most of the "people" here ignored what was going on, but the loud squawling drove Tucker to wincing.

The alien mother kept tweaking a complicated breathing apparatus on her child's nose. Ear. Whatever it was. Tucker thought at first the mother was trying to get the kid to stop crying, but every time she twisted the device, the child went into greater and greater distress.

Why was she taunting him? It? Was this some kind of bizarre alien mothering ritual? Drive your child crazy with suffocation and it'll behave?

He shifted in his seat and glanced at T'Pol and the constable. How much longer was she going to take? She seemed to be doing all the talking. What good was that?

The mother twisted her child's breathing device again. The poor thing howled in agony.

A few people around him shifted just from the noise, but no one interfered. What kind of people were these? To stand by and witness child abuse without a flicker? This was what awaited humanity in the open galaxy?

Here came T'Pol. She motioned to Tucker, who quickly got up and hurried across the field of feet and tails to her side. By the time he reached her, she was already speaking into her communicator.

"T'Pol to Archer."

On the com unit, the captain responded almost immediately. "Go ahead."

The wail of the distressed child cut off any chance at conversation. Tucker turned to the mother, unable to control himself any longer. "Hey—"

T'Pol ignored his concern and continued speaking to the captain. "Central Security claims to have no record of Klaang. But they told me about an enclave on level nineteen where Klingons have been known to go. Something about live food."

"Where on level nineteen?" the captain asked.

"The easternmost subsection. By the geothermal shafts."

"I'll meet you there as soon as I can. Archer out."

The alien child was hysterical now. Tucker's innards squirmed as the mother disconnected the breathing tube entirely. The child was suffocating!

Tucker bolted forward. "What are you doing! Leave that kid alone!"

T'Pol was right after him and seized him by the arm. "Don't get involved."

"Do you see what she's doing? He's going to suffocate!"

"They're Lorillians. Before the age of four, they can only breathe methyloxide." She paused, watching the mother and child as the little one began finally to grow quiet and begin breathing on his own, without the device. "The mother is simply weaning her son."

Tucker inhaled deeply in empathy. "Could've fooled me. . . ."

"Humans can't refrain from drawing conclusions," T'Pol scolded. "You should learn to objectify other cultures so you can determine when to interfere and when *not* to."

Tucker glanced back at the child. He knew he'd made a mistake, but that was all it was. He didn't like being lectured.

He followed her into the open stretch of walkways and tubes leading toward the upper levels. "Well, hey, Sub-Commander," he told her, "next time I see somebody backing you into a corner and taking a switchblade to your ribs, I'll know to wait a few minutes just in case it's a dance. Do you feel like somebody's following us? I feel like we're being watched. Do you get that feeling? I do. . . ."

"Do you think they're all right?"

"No way to know yet."

"They don't like each other."

"I don't think T'Pol would let anything happen to Tucker, no matter how they feel about each other."

Archer led Hoshi through a forbidding trade complex much more desolate and eerie than the central cluster. Deep grinding noises from the power generators far below echoed through damp floors that creaked under their feet. He kept Hoshi close behind him as they skimmed past rows of burping geothermic ducts that constantly vented violent shots of steam.

And they were completely alone.

"Isn't an 'enclave' supposed to have people?" Hoshi nervously asked.

" 'Enclave' can mean a lot of things," Archer comforted, but he kept his eyes open. The place looked empty, but that also could mean a lot of things.

"T'Pol said something about 'live' food," Hoshi went on, quite spooked. "I don't see any restaurants. . . ."

Archer started to answer, but drew up short instead as a flicker of movement caught his eye in the industrial distance. Klingons!

"Excuse me!" he shouted. "Hello! Excuse me!"

The Klingons moved away from them.

"Hoshi!" he snapped.

She flinched, then shouted, *"Ha'quj jeg!"*

But there was only silence. The movement stopped. The shadows sagged back to stillness.

"They looked Klingon to me," she said, suddenly breathless and completely jittery.

Archer grunted a dissatisfied response and snapped up his communicator. "Archer to T'Pol." After a moment, when no answer came, he repeated, "T'Pol, come in."

Anxiety rose as no answer came. Hoshi shivered at his side. "Maybe we should get back to where there are more people. . . ."

"There are plenty of people right here."

He drew his plasma pistol. The movement frightened her.

"Stay behind me," he warned.

They moved into the deep purpose shadows along the path leading to where the Klingons had disappeared. Above, a spiderweb of age-old metal drums, bridges, archways, and tubes threaded the darkness. Steam billowed from the geothermal ducts, obscuring every step before they took it.

There was someone here. He felt the shifting gazes of the shadows and pounding machinery. Silence would be better than this constant grinding and drumming.

They passed too close to a geothermal duct just as it blew its top. A mushroom of gray-white steam burped from the depths and separated Archer from Hoshi for a critical instant.

He glanced behind, but she was lost in steam.

A piece of a shadow burst toward him—Hoshi's hand flashed in the cloud and she screamed, only steps from Archer, but though he reached out, she slipped away.

He whirled full about and took aim—what could he do? Shoot her?

In that instant of hesitation, he was attacked from two sides by a now-familiar dappled team who moved like insects. Suliban!

His pistol flew from his hand at a single blow. His fingers went numb, and he stumbled. He lashed out with the other fist and landed a solid strike on a surface that collapsed—a lung or stomach—and seconds turned into punches. One of the attackers fell back.

The other, though, made use of his partner as a distraction. Archer spun to keep fighting, but his arms were yanked behind him so violently that he gasped with pain and arched his back. In the steam, Hoshi cried out again. At least she was alive!

Frantic, he let out a kick, but failed to connect. His hip twisted. A shot of pain rushed up his side. His attackers took the advantage. With a single gasp of protest, Jonathan Archer was dragged into the dark depths as if swallowed by a giant burrowing animal.

CHAPTER 10

A STEAMY MAZE . . . VERTICAL, DIAGONAL, HORIZONTAL tubes, bridges . . .

Archer fought to stay conscious. One of the Suliban must've landed a blow on his head or neck. He strained to see Hoshi. She was behind him, but no longer safe there.

They had succeeded in making their presence known, whether that would turn out to be good or bad. Rather than finding someone, they had succeeded in being found. He took that as progress.

They were being pushed right along at a daunting pace for his aching thigh. He forced his leg to keep moving. Couldn't let it freeze up on him. Might have to run.

One of the two Suliban who pushed them along had his plasma pistol. He caught glimpses of it, just enough to tempt him every few seconds. He wanted the weapon back, and pummeled himself mentally for losing it to them. He had handed his enemy an advantage. Rule number one broken.

Sweat drained down his face. The surroundings were

getting hotter and steamier, though the Suliban didn't seem affected at all—

What was that? An energy field?

Archer blinked as a fizzing light half blinded him. He fought to adjust.

T'Pol! And Trip—in a box of some kind, with a force field locking them in. Like Hoshi, alive. Now that he knew for sure they were being stalked, Archer got a burst of relief at seeing them. Where were Reed and Mayweather?

He winced as the Suliban operatives yanked him to a stop. Hoshi bumped his right arm. One of the Suliban worked a handheld device that caused the energy field to snap down. Then that same Suliban reached for Hoshi.

Archer tried to get between them, but there was no fighting the strength of the individual who had him by both arms behind his back. This one had figured out that Archer's leg was hurt and he could be held off balance.

As the Suliban with the device pulled Hoshi inside the chamber and left her with T'Pol and Tucker, Archer noticed that these two weren't dressed the same as the two who had infiltrated the *Enterprise.* Of course, that didn't mean they weren't the same two. He couldn't tell from their mottled faces, or make out any individuality at all.

Archer waited to be put inside. Instead, the Suliban stepped out and raised the electrical shield again. From inside, Tucker stepped forward toward Archer, but there was no hope to break through the force field. T'Pol gave him no such concern. Instead, she seemed to be saying with her eyes *I told you so.*

Angry and aching, Archer let himself be led away without further struggle. He sensed a chance for answers now, if not the ones he wanted.

What would be done with his crew? Would they be interrogated? Pressured?

The Suliban pulled him down a conduit to some steps, then down the steps. He had to duck twice, bumped his head once on something he never saw, and was drawn through three locked doors and a small hatch. Thoroughly disoriented by the time they stopped, Archer found himself in a chamber with beds, computers, piles of clothing, tables and chairs, and clutter.

He looked around critically and got an idea about this place. He knew a secret subversive base when he saw one. Were the Suliban dissidents? Against whom?

Or more pointedly, were *these* Suliban dissidents?

The two Suliban finally let him have his arms back. Without a word or gesture, they turned and left him alone in this chamber—which probably meant there was no easy way out. Judging from the way they came in, he might be lost down here for weeks before he found his way to the surface.

"You're looking for Klaang," a female voice said in perfect English. "Why?"

Archer turned, looked. Neither of the Suliban had come back or spoken. Who had?

"Who the hell are you?" he demanded coldly.

The shadows behind a stack of boxes shifted. A woman stepped out. Strikingly lovely and definitely human, the woman strode toward him, studying him as she came.

"My name is Sarin. Tell me about the people who took Klaang off your ship."

"I was hoping you could tell me," Archer reversed. "They looked a lot like your friends outside."

She stepped toward him. "Where were you taking him?"

"How come you don't look like your friends?" he asked, instead of giving her anything.

She was uncomfortably close now. "Would you prefer I did?" she asked in a sultry tone.

Oh, brother. This dame had seen too many steamy movies. She had the sticky dialogue down pat, not to mention the unoriginal seductive stare and liquid lips. What did they take him for?

Stick to business.

"What I'd prefer," he attempted again, "is that you give me Klaang back."

"So you could take him where?"

"Home. We were just taking him home."

Sarin was now inches away. Less. She seemed to be gauging him. He was returning the favor.

"You'd better be careful," Archer murmured. "I'm a lot bigger than you are."

She moved until they were very close and her breath brushed his cheek. "If you're thinking of harming me, I'd advise against it."

She ran her hand along his jawline.

"What're you doing?" he asked, as if he didn't know.

"Why were you taking Klaang home?"

"Y'know," he said instead, "under different circumstances, I might be flattered by this, but . . ."

Sarin came up on her toes and pressed her lips to his, forcefully and with purpose. Archer coolly accepted what was happening and bothered to relax enough that she might get discouraged sooner. With his ship on the line and his crew in a cage, he didn't much care how seductive she wanted to playact.

She got whatever she wanted—or didn't—and stepped back rather abruptly. Her face began to melt.

A moment later, she was Suliban. Archer grimaced in disgust.

"That's never happened before," he offered.

"I've been given the ability to measure trust," she said, "but it requires close contact."

Maybe next time they could just shake hands. He tried to imagine her smooching T'Pol, and shook that image away before it took hold.

"You're Suliban," he said, giving her a pretense of the shock she was probably going for.

"I *was* a member of the Cabal," Sarin said, "but not anymore. The price of evolution is too high."

"Evolution?"

Carefully, she moved away, no longer meeting his eyes. "Some of my people are so anxious to 'improve' themselves that they've lost perspective."

"So you know I'm not lying to you," Archer vectored back to the point. "Now what?"

"Klaang was carrying a message to his people."

"How do you know that?"

"I gave it to him."

"What kind of message?"

"The Suliban have been staging attacks within the Klingon Empire," she told him. "Making it appear that one faction is attacking another. Klaang was bringing proof of this to his High Council. Without that proof, the Empire could be thrown into chaos."

"Why would the Suliban want that?" Archer asked, following her and keeping her from turning away. He knew guilt when he saw it, and was determined to get answers before she changed her mind or had an attack of regret.

"The Cabal doesn't make decisions on its own," she went on, more anxious to tell him things. "They're simply soldiers fighting a temporal cold war."

"Temporal? You've lost me."

"They're taking orders from the distant future."

The announcement stopped Archer in his tracks. He ended up leaning on his bad leg, enduring shots of pain through his hip, but the strange concept held him still. "What?"

In his periphery he saw a movement on the ceiling and flinched. Only a shot of steam from a crack.

Temporal cold war . . .

Sarin turned fully to face him, now firm with conviction. If she had harbored any doubts, they were gone.

"We can help you find Klaang," she said quickly. "But we don't have a starship. You'll have to take us with you!"

A blinding flash of blue light discharged between them. A computer station at Archer's elbow exploded into shards and drove him sideways. He reached for Sarin and pulled her out of the blast area.

Another weapon blast struck even closer. Two Suliban skittered across the ceiling, firing weapons at them!

It didn't take a genius to understand that the secret base had been breached and these weren't the same two Suliban who had brought him here.

Sarin's Suliban came streaking in from a doorway, firing as they ran, but the other Suliban seemed to have physical advantages. They skimmed the walls and ceiling like insects.

All hell broke loose. Archer dragged Sarin toward the

way they'd come in, assuming she would have the sense to lead him out through those tubes—

"Get us out!" Archer choked.

In fact, she had a shortcut. Five seconds later, they were out in the main access level, being sprayed by geothermals and burned by the fritzing electrical screen that blocked off the *Enterprise* landing party. Behind them, the battle raged—Suliban against Suliban.

One of Sarin's operatives fell dead just inches behind Archer, while the other exchanged hand-weapon fire with the two attackers. Sarin raised a weapon now that Archer hadn't even known she possessed, and began returning fire, blocking blast after blast that might've taken Archer's head off.

Sarin's other operative followed them out, rushing frantically along a bridge, firing as he went. He blasted one of the two attackers, but was caught in crossfire and killed by the second invader.

That left Archer and Sarin on their own—and Archer had no weapon! His team was armed, but they couldn't get through the force field. He had to break that force field!

The Suliban attacker, the remaining one, had the same idea. He drove Archer and Sarin into hiding with his wild firing, then opened on the force field with the *Enterprise* crewmen behind it. They dove for cover, but there wasn't any. All they could do was crouch with each other as the field disrupted in blinding displays of free energy.

At Archer's side, Sarin took the initiative and stood clear. She fired openly at the attacker's body and blew him off his feet. With that window of opportunity, she rushed to the control panel of the force field and worked it with some kind of code.

The field fell! The crew flooded out, Tucker first. T'Pol pushed Hoshi before her.

Sarin yanked open a panel that turned out to be a locker. She started handing the crew their plasma pistols!

Archer briefly connected with Tucker—just a reassuring glance—and they were off running.

"Where is your vessel?" Sarin asked.

"On the roof! Docking port three!"

"Captain!" Hoshi cried, and pointed at the underside of a diagonal conduit high over the ground. Two more Suliban, defying gravity, crawled along the pipe!

"This way!" Sarin called.

As she led them in a completely confusing direction, one of the Suliban dropped and landed only a pace from Archer.

He lashed out, and the Suliban sprang out of reach and out of sight with a heightened agility that startled even Sarin.

But here were two more Suliban—dressed like Sarin's associates. *On our side?* Yes! They were firing at the other Suliban!

How many people were in Sarin's subversive splinter group? Right now Archer wanted dozens, hundreds.

Flashes of weapons fire illuminated the distance. The Starfleet team plowed forward after Sarin, ducking and running, navigating the wild jungle of pipes and buttresses.

Sarin reached a massive vertical tube, hit a control, and opened a hatch that Archer was relieved to see, because there was no way to climb this monolith. A large pipe opened before them. Inside was a circular platform a few feet above the deck. Archer spun to pile Hoshi into the hole while Tucker acted as rearguard.

What about Reed and Mayweather?

He reached for T'Pol.

Weapons fire streaked in from hundreds of feet away.

"Trip!" Archer called, and shoved the engineer onto the platform, then piled in after him. Under them, the platform began to rumble and shift with the rush of thermal energy. Sarin was doing something with a control box. Was this an elevator?

"Come on!" Archer waved, but his voice was snatched away by a thermal rush.

Sarin moved toward the platform. She reached out to climb aboard. A blast struck her square in the back.

A Suliban stood across the area, his weapon trained on her. He fired again just as his eyes met Archer's.

Sarin fell hard. The points of impact on her back glowed and sizzled as they burned their way through her writhing body.

Archer launched off the platform, followed by Tucker. Tucker provided covering fire and drove the Suliban back while Archer knelt at Sarin's side.

The Suliban took cover behind an outcropping of twisted pipes, but he was more persistent than the others and didn't run. Archer's mind flashed on his moment of contact with the single Suliban, and he recognized something in this individual's eyes, his manner, his drive. Unlike the others, who had ducked and hidden with more relish than they had fought, this one had a stake in whatever was happening.

Archer glanced over again and memorized the patterns of dappling on this Suliban's face.

But beneath his hands, the female Suliban was dying.

"Find Klaang," Sarin murmured raggedly.

Mercifully, she lost consciousness as the wounds in

her body continued to glow, burn, and grow, eating her from the inside out.

"Trip!" Archer bolted to his feet. He hoped it would be quick for Sarin. He could give her no more now.

He motioned for Tucker, and together they jumped back onto the trembling platform. Archer slid the hatch shut.

The moment he did that, the platform blasted upward through the shaft, driving them to their knees, propelled by a rolling pillar of steam.

In seconds the hot steam was blown away by an arctic blast. Archer forced his eyes open and saw snow blanketing the landing dock. They'd made it!

The platform shot up and stopped a full two feet over the dock. The Starfleet team was thrown into a pile, but alive. Steam blasted out in all directions under them, billowing into the frozen air.

Still covered with sweat, Archer pulled his team into the frigid snow. "Let's go!" he called over the whine of wind and blowing ice.

"Where's the pod?" Hoshi called.

"Over here!" Tucker waved and pointed.

T'Pol, though, called louder over the wind and pointed in a different direction. "No, this way!"

Archer weighed the two options, then picked T'Pol's direction. She was the only one who had ever been here before. He made the bet and pointed. "Come on!"

As the four of them headed toward an obscured shape with two lights that might indeed be the shuttle, Archer bent against the wind, endured the sweat freezing on his cheeks, and brought the communicator up, flipping it as he ran. "Lieutenant Reed, this is Archer! Come in!"

"zzzzzzkkkkkggggaaazzzk."

"We're up on the roof! You need to get up here as quickly as possible! Where are you? Emergency evacuation! Reed!"

The communicator buzzed frantically. Someone was definitely trying to get through to him. Where were they? How deeply had they wandered into that steamy maze?

The storm was getting worse. The landing deck was turning into a skating rink. Archer fell twice, Tucker once, and the women stumbled into each other like skittering ducks before the shuttlepod took shape before them in the white fume.

Unintelligible sounds continued to burst from his communicator. He left it open, hoping to hear something that would give him a clue he could follow somehow to get Reed and Mayweather out of the complex, and all of them away from these attacks.

Suliban soldiers appeared only seconds after Archer and his shipmates skidded onto the frozen deck. Time seemed to crawl when a blast rocketed past him.

The wind began to clear. Blowing snow flattened into a sea, and the docking platform opened before them—empty! The obscured shape had been nothing but an approach shield!

"Great!" Hoshi blurted.

"Like I said," Tucker shouted, "it's over there!"

Another blast of weapons fire sliced the air. Archer ducked and ordered, "Weapons!"

They had to cross the deck again. And now the Suliban had found them! Even in the now-rising snowstorm, Archer caught a glimpse of his determined counterpart, the one Suliban who wouldn't be put off, and whose resolve gave substance to the others behind him.

But there was distance between them. Archer was resolved, too, and worked to use the blowing snow as a shield. If it could obscure a whole platform, then he could make it obscure his team.

"Down! Get low, everybody! Form a single file!"

He tried to imagine what the Suliban would be seeing. Lower—lower—and keep moving steadily. Sporadic movement would gain more attention.

They kept searching for the shuttle, this time following Tucker through the storm of snow and weapons fire, firing all the way. Deep red plasma bullets streaked across the platform toward the place where the Suliban shots were coming from. Though the Suliban were moving toward them, Archer sensed they were being held back by his and Tucker's shots. T'Pol was more reserved, taking shots more carefully, but she, too, was succeeding in driving them back. Hoshi was just skittering like a bird across the ice, intent on their target. She had a weapon, but she also knew she was of little use with it. Probably smart to let the trained officers handle that detail, Archer noted as the moments rushed past.

His single-file trick was working. Suliban shots were going wild behind them. Then they corrected their error forward, and the team was forced to scatter. Hot blue beams cut between them, driving them away from each other.

A darkened form, sheeted and blistered with ice, suddenly flashed with blue energy before them. The shuttlepod! The Suliban weapons fire lit up the skin of the pod and gave the Starfleet team a clear beacon to safety.

T'Pol circled around Archer and pounded on the shuttle window. Why was she doing that?

The emergency hatch began to crack open, popped out a few inches, and swung wider. Air gushed with equalization and temperature change.

Archer tried to reach the shuttle, but a crackle of blue energy raked the hull and drove him back into the swirling snow. His face and hands were numb with cold now. Where was Hoshi? He'd lost sight of her!

The Suliban were closing in. He knew that without even looking. He'd be doing the same thing.

"Hoshi!"

"Captain?" her voice was weak, but not far.

Shivering now, he forced his legs to keep moving away from the shuttle and toward her voice. Behind a wall over there, Tucker was firing steadily at something he could obviously see. The cover gave Archer time to find Hoshi in the roiling white storm. Without saying anything, he took her arm and pulled her along back the way he had just come.

Where were his footprints? He had just come this way, but the trail was already erased.

A mechanical roar directly overhead shook him to his boots. He pushed Hoshi down and tried to see what new method of attack the Suliban had invented. An aircraft—an alien craft launching from the port! Only its running lights showed through the blowing snow. Its great gush of thruster exhaust caused a frozen hell down here.

Archer pulled his eyes away from the transport overhead and squinted through the miasma toward the place where the Suliban shots had come from.

They'd stopped. The Suliban were driven down by the thruster exhaust. But the exhaust did one favor here and executed a problem over there—T'Pol was directly under the exhaust. The force knocked her off her feet and blew her across the deck. She had been near the shuttlepod and now she was way over there, shifting and dazed, alone, unarmed.

The Suliban soldiers and their leader rose out of the exhaust stream as the big ship moved away from the pad. They saw T'Pol. A clear target.

"Get to the ship!" Archer shouted at Hoshi over the wind.

Luckily she wasn't the heroic type and did as he ordered.

Archer thrust himself up on his aching legs and made himself obvious. He snapped his pistol up just as the Suliban leader noticed him. Without looking for cover, he ran furiously across the tarmac, directly toward the Suliban, firing as he ran.

One of the Suliban was struck by a lucky shot—lucky only because most of his plasma bullets were being sucked sideways by the wind vortex on these open flats. One more down.

The leader and the other soldier took cover. Archer reached T'Pol's weapon, scooped it up without missing a step, and kept on with his direct assault.

"Go!" he called to her.

"*Enterprise* needs its captain!" she called back. "Give me the weapon!"

"I said, *go!*"

To her credit, she hesitated another moment. During that moment he struck her with a look so forceful that she must have realized she wouldn't be changing his mind. This was no time for a discussion.

Archer broke the contact, raised the second weapon,

and began firing both as T'Pol ran behind him toward the shuttle.

He glanced back to gauge her progress and saw the shuttlepod hatch open again for her. Reed was reaching for her! Archer spotted Mayweather warming up the helm. They were already aboard!

A flush of relief numbed Archer's whole body. His team was intact!

As Reed pulled T'Pol inside, Archer moved backward toward the shuttle, firing constantly. The pistol in his left hand began to cool. Losing power!

The Suliban leader waved his hand. The Suliban broke apart from each other, forcing Archer to divide his target. The leader had figured out what to do, a simple but effective maneuver.

Archer was closer to the shuttle now, close enough for a good leap if he could only turn around, but he had to keep shooting. He aimed slightly to his left at a moving form.

From his right, a blue shot streaked in. His leg folded under him, burning and quivering. A moment later, the blinding pain struck full out.

A tangle of movement confused him. Reed, right overhead, firing into the snow!

Trip Tucker appeared at his side and pulled him through the hatch. Archer did everything he could to save himself and them from further torment, but he could barely think over the searing pain in his thigh. His thoughts piled together. Nothing made sense. He dug his shoulder into Tucker and accepted the support from his friend, who could do nothing for him, not here, like this.

"The starboard thruster's down!" Mayweather spat.

"Ignore it." T'Pol, almost excited. "Take us up."

Hoshi's face appeared in his closing periphery. She looked small, distant.

"Open a channel." T'Pol again.

The surge of acceleration made Archer's mind swarm like bees in the sky. The lower half of his body sizzled, as if he were being fried in a skillet. He tried to move, to sit up—

"Sub-Commander T'Pol to *Enterprise.*"

"Go ahead," the voice on the com responded.

"We'll be docking in a few minutes. Have Dr. Phlox meet us in decon."

"Acknowledged. Is someone wounded?"

Archer tried to speak, to protest that he could stand, work, take them back to the ship, and go on with their mission to find Klaang . . . the Klingons . . . he had to . . .

"Your pitch is too low. Bring the nose up."

The pod rocked and turned in the wind. The port nacelle struck a branch and skidded into the snow. No, it was sand . . .

"It's okay. You've almost got it. Try again."

The ship skittered on the sand and rose over open water, airborne again, wavering.

"I can't do it!"

Dad, I can't keep the ship in the air! Why can't I do it right?

"Yes, you can. Take her up, straight and steady."

The ship skidded into a sand dune, bruised and lifeless.

"Damn!" Archer gushed.

Dad came to his side.

"You can't be afraid of the wind," he said. "Learn to trust it."

Archer turned and looked up onto the dune. T'Pol stood watching him and his father as they worked the model ship and tried to make it fly. What was she doing here?

"The captain is injured," she said. "I'm taking command of the *Enterprise.*"

Dad didn't seem surprised. Why not?

CHAPTER 11

"YOU'RE NOT IN COMMAND YET. DON'T GET AHEAD OF yourself."

"The captain is incapacitated. My action is logical."

"That's what you think."

Trip Tucker shed his wet field jacket and dumped it on the hangar deck beside the scarred and steaming shuttle-pod, leaving him in a clammy, snowcaked uniform. He watched with dismay as the medics disappeared into the turbolift with the captain on an antigrav gurney. Things weren't supposed to be this way. Who would design a scenario like this? The captain incapacitated two days into the mission?

What kind of bolt had struck him? The wound had been chewing away at itself all the way back here, as if burning from the inside out. Tucker's innards twisted at the memory of it, of Archer's face as consciousness faded, giving the only relief from what must've been torture.

He wracked his mind for signs that the whole episode had been a trap engineered from inside this ship. Had

T'Pol given Archer false information about the Klingon's activities? Everything stemmed from her. Now she was an inch from making the next command decisions.

"He saved your life," he told her. "You owe him a buffer zone. Give him time to come out of the sedatives they just gave him."

"Dr. Phlox is working on the wound," T'Pol said. "The captain will see to himself, as we all must. Command responsibility is now mine. Even you cannot dispute it."

"Watch me. I'm going to check on the captain."

He started toward the exit.

"You haven't been scanned for contaminants," T'Pol called. "Tucker! The safety of the rest of the crew!"

That stopped him. Damn, it did. He couldn't much comment on her responsibilities if he didn't oblige his own.

"Hell, all right . . ."

"Is this really necessary?"

Tucker shifted his feet uneasily as he and T'Pol stood side by side in the decon chamber, still in their wet uniforms, now bathed in ultraviolet light.

Dr. Phlox was here instead of sickbay—probably a good sign for the captain.

"The other scans were negative," he said. "You two, unfortunately, were exposed to a protocystian spore. I've loaded the appropriate decon-gel into compartment B."

Tucker groaned and began to strip out of his uniform. Beside him, T'Pol did the same.

"Tell Mr. Mayweather to prepare to leave orbit," T'Pol said to the doctor.

"How's the captain?" Tucker bluntly reminded, insisting that she not forget the weight of what she was about to do.

"I'm treating his wound," Phlox said.

"Will he be all right?"

"Eventually."

A metal slat slid shut, cutting off Tucker and T'Pol from the rest of the ship. They each turned to a locker, opened it, and deposited their contaminated uniforms inside. Tucker tossed his in. T'Pol used the hook.

Tucker stripped down to his shorts. T'Pol had some sort of a cropped T-shirt top on as well as her underwear. She opened compartment B and pulled out two beakers of gelatin, deep blue and gooey.

Without comment she turned to him, handed him a beaker, and they began spreading the goop on each other. The phosphorescent gel glowed in the ultraviolet light, turning them both into Halloween characters.

"Correct me if I'm wrong," Tucker began, "but aren't you just kind of an 'observer' on this mission? I don't remember anyone telling me you were a member of Starfleet."

"My Vulcan rank supersedes yours," she said.

He bristled. "Apples and oranges. This is an Earth vessel. You're in no position to take command."

"As soon as we're through here, I'll contact Ambassador Soval. He'll speak to your superiors, and I'm certain they'll support my authority in this situation."

Tucker clamped his lips. If she made the call, this mission was over.

"You must really be proud of yourself. You can put an end to this mission while the captain's still unconscious in sickbay. You won't even have to look him in the eye."

"Your precious 'cargo' was stolen," she said irritably. "Three Suliban, perhaps more, were killed, and Captain

Archer has been seriously wounded. It seems to me this mission has put an end to itself. Turn around."

"Let's say you're right," he went on, reining in his combativeness just long enough to get this out. "Let's say we screwed up, just like you always knew we would.

"It's still a pretty good bet that whoever blew that hole in the captain's leg is connected somehow to the people who took Klaang."

"I fail to see your point."

"Captain Archer deserves the chance to see this through. If you knew him, you'd realize that's what he's about. He needs to finish what he starts. His daddy was the same way."

But he never got to finish. That was your fault, too, you people.

"You obviously share the captain's belief," she said, "that my people were responsible for impeding Henry Archer's accomplishments."

At least Tucker knew he wasn't being too subtle.

"He only wanted to see his engine fly. They never even gave him the chance to fail. And here *you* are, thirty years later, proving just how consistent you Vulcans can be."

They fell silent as each took a towel and began wiping off the blue gel, now that it had set into a film.

"Tell you the truth," Tucker continued after a few moments, "we don't know why you're here. There's nothing to 'observe,' so who stuck us with you? But you notice we accepted you. Nobody's been giving you dirty looks, 'cept maybe me once in a while. That's how we silly humans are. We trust first, and ask each other to come up to it. Maybe you don't."

T'Pol pulled the congealed film from her lips and

cheeks, and revealed soft puckering around her eyes. Worry? Guilt?

"You know nothing about me," she protested without much enthusiasm.

Tucker grunted with the irony of her statement. "Funny, isn't it? We trust you anyway. Odd, silly humans . . . You can follow along behind every Vulcan who came before you, but I don't hold much for that kind of life. I wonder if you've got the steel to go off on your own. Maybe . . . The captain must see *something* in you, or he wouldn't have accepted you in his command line. He didn't have to do that, you know. What do you think he saw? Youth? Grace?"

"Those aren't command traits," she said. This time her voice was very quiet."

"Hell, no, they aren't," Tucker shot back. "Not even your 'Vulcan' rank is enough to get you what you've got here. You wouldn't have it if Jonathan hadn't given you the chance you're denying him. We're 'only' humans . . . but we gave you the same trust we give each other. Now the captain's asking you to return it. You got the guts?"

She didn't respond. She had cut herself off from the conversation.

Tucker reached into another locker and pulled out a fresh T-shirt. "I guess we'll see," he said.

The ship was flying now. Pretty against the sky.

Jonathan Archer opened his eyes, gritted his teeth against a sudden shot of pain, and looked down at his legs.

He was lying, partially reclined, on a biobed. Dr. Phlox was at work on his thigh wound, removing what looked like a disembodied liver from the leg.

Underneath the liver, the wound was reddened, but sealed.

"Very nice," Phlox commented. "Very nice. Your myofibers are fusing beautifully!"

Archer moved his arms and flexed his neck muscles. "How long have I been . . ."

"Less than six hours. I thought it best to keep you sedated while the osmotic eel cauterized your wound."

Phlox appreciated his glossy little pet, then deposited the thing into a pot of fluid.

Archer looked at the creature, now happily swimming around, and reserved judgment. "Thanks."

He started to ask about the landing party—was everyone else all right? But Trip Tucker and T'Pol entered, answering part of his question here and now.

"How're you doing, Captain?" Trip asked immediately. Relief showed in his face to see Archer awake and lucid.

"That depends," Archer said. "What's been going on for the last six hours?"

Tucker didn't say anything. What did that mean?

T'Pol raised her chin a little and announced. "As your highest ranking officer, I assumed command while you were incapacitated."

Archer's stomach sank. "Are we underway?"

Tucker nodded.

To T'Pol, Archer coldly accused, "You didn't waste much time, did you?"

She didn't respond, but turned to Phlox. "Is he fit to resume command?"

"As long as he returns for more eel therapy tomorrow."

Archer ignored her and looked at Tucker. "How long till we get back to Earth?"

"Earth, sir?"

Was that a hint of a smile?

T'Pol turned back to them. "We're currently tracking the Suliban vessel that left Rigel shortly after you were injured."

Skeptical and surprised, Archer asked, "You got their . . . plasma decay rate?"

"With Mr. Tucker's assistance, I modified your sensors. We now have the resolution to detect their warp trail."

"What happened to 'This is a foolish mission'?"

"It *is* a foolish mission," she insisted. "The Suliban are clearly a hostile race with technology far superior to yours. But, as acting captain . . . I was obligated to anticipate *your* wishes."

Well, well, well. Had something changed in Archer's dreams? "As acting captain," he echoed, "you could've done whatever the hell you wanted to do."

Her cheeks flushed olive—just enough to notice—but she didn't offer any explanations or comments on what he had just said to her.

"I should return to the bridge," was all she said.

"Dismissed."

Archer had more to say, but he let her go. Whatever had happened, it was hard enough on her to buck the Vulcan trend. Renewed hope surged up. He hadn't lost the mission yet.

Trip Tucker waited until the door closed, then looked at Archer. With significance, he said, "Modifying the sensors *was* her idea, sir."

Archer let his head sink back on the cushion. "Why would she do that? Go against the wishes of whoever designed her position here?"

"It just might be," Tucker said with a twinkle, "you're

having more effect on her than they are. Whoever *they* are."

"Have you and Reed found out anything?"

"She's clean and normal right up until she gets the scholarship that put her in Soval's office. Then, her records start getting real terse and kind of vague."

"Could be just the logging style of that office," Archer mentioned. "Details never were very important to Soval."

"Or it could be a masking technique," Tucker said. "Got to admit, I was knocked over when she decided to pursue."

"It's not what a spy would do, is it?"

"No . . . sir, could it be she's a spy and even she doesn't know it?"

"If she doesn't know it, then I don't care one way or the other. As long as she knows who she works for here and now."

Tucker paced around the end of the bed. "She might work for you . . . except we picked up log echoes of several messages going back and forth between Soval and Admiral Forrest just before she was assigned."

Archer narrowed his eyes in thought. "I didn't think Soval and Forrest had that much to say to each other."

"You think they're up to something?" Tucker asked. "And she's the something?"

"Or *we're* the something. All of us, together. I know Forrest. He's not likely to have me watched. If he agreed to a Vulcan plant, there must be a different reason. Completely different."

"They wouldn't tell you?"

"I'd be the last person they'd tell. Trip . . . what do you think of this . . . maybe the Vulcans really don't know if they can be around humans and function for decades upon decades. Maybe Soval finally wants to know, once and for all, if we can exist together in hostile space and come out productive."

"You mean they're testing us?"

Archer thought about that, then dismissed it. "I doubt it. They know everything there is to know about humanity. All you have to do is look at history. It's all there. We don't hide anything, even the worst things. Humans aren't a mystery. But . . . *Vulcans* are still a mystery, even to each other. They don't step out of that box very often, and they're about to be kicked right out. It could be they're testing themselves. And they're using her to do it."

"T'Pol's the guinea pig?" Tucker blurted. "They want to see how *she'll* do? I'll be damned!"

"And it worked," Archer said. "Her technical expertise and ability to stay cool, side by side with my irrational leaps of anger and whatever else I've got . . . it worked. We came out of our first big test as a human-Vulcan team."

"I'll be damned . . . How can you confirm any of this?"

"I probably can't. All I can do is keep going forward with nothing to hide. A spy's no good if you've got nothing to hide."

"How 'bout that . . . T'Pol's the lab animal. What do you know!" Tucker slapped the end of the bed with a victorious hand, then recoiled. "Sorry! Did I hurt you?"

Archer leaned back, put his arms behind his head, and luxuriated. "Trip, I don't think anybody can hurt me anymore today."

"What are the symptoms of frostbite?"

Hoshi Sato picked at her fingertips. Behind her complaints, the sensor console was making a strange and frantic *ping* every few seconds.

Lieutenant Reed didn't offer her a sympathetic glance, but did explain, "Your appendages blister, peel, turn gangrenous."

"I think I have frostbite."

Ah, well. He moved closer to her, glad he didn't have to cross in front of T'Pol in the command chair. "Let me see . . . Dr. Phlox may have to amputate."

Hoshi frowned. "I never had to worry about frostbite in Brazil."

Before he could respond, the *pings* became suddenly more frantic and closer together.

"They're getting too far ahead of us," Ensign Mayweather said, watching the helm with frustration.

"Match their speed," T'Pol said flatly.

Mayweather glanced helplessly at Reed, then declared, "I'm not authorized to go beyond four-four."

T'Pol tapped a button.

"Engineering," Tucker's voice answered.

"Mr. Tucker, would you please give the helmsman permission to go to warp four point five."

"It's okay, Travis. I'll keep an eye on the engines."

Reed watched Mayweather, but couldn't tell whether the helmsman liked or disliked what he was now doing. The ship surged under them, physically and with great confidence. The *ping*ing slowed down to a normal rhythm and volume. The sensors were much happier.

There was a certain irony in T'Pol's being the one to give the order to go to four-five. Reed tried not to be affected by such trivialities, but some rites of passage should belong to the captain alone. Yet, without consideration, the Vulcan woman had seized the privilege for herself. And the glory, if any came?

He respected the uniform, as he must, but her presence here was the culmination of a dire prediction by Trip Tucker. Tucker's instincts had proven correct, or partially. In fact, this woman had bothered to execute the captain's plans instead of her own.

Still, his investigation had turned up a strange trail of communiqués culminating in her assignment here. The captain had chosen not to question the trail, but to push them all farther down it. Now T'Pol was, perhaps, still being manipulated, but by Jonathan Archer.

Very nice. Reed rocked on his heels. Very nice indeed.

"Archer to bridge."

Reed relieved Hoshi of the need to use her poor fingers by pushing the intercom himself. "Yes, sir, Reed here."

"Tucker says we just accomplished four-five. I'd have liked to have been there for that."

T'Pol glanced at Reed, but let him do the talking.

"You are here, sir, in all our spirits. We wouldn't have been here at all if not for you."

"The farther in the future they are, the more crazy and dangerous it is that they would be doing these things. While it has marginal effects on people here, it could completely change their own time. So what do they want?"

Jonathan Archer took tentative steps as he circumnavigated the table in his office. His leg was tingling from the knee to the hip. Still not good.

"Trip . . . give me a hand."

Trip Tucker rushed to him from the couch and eagerly

helped him back into the office chair. Beside them, stars streaked by the portal at high warp. Archer felt out of commission, wearing only his T-shirt and nonreg trousers, but he knew he had to give himself another hour to come out of the doctor's funny sedative. He seemed to have the time. They were in hot pursuit, but only matching the speed of the people they were pursuing. They didn't, after all, want to catch them—not quite yet. They wanted to be led somewhere first.

Warp four point five . . .

"It's possible there's something about time travel we don't understand," Archer suggested.

"I'd say the odds for that are good," Tucker grumbled as he stuffed a pillow under the captain's bad leg and bothered to fluff it. He straightened and surveyed his work. "Feel better?"

"Fine, I'm fine, Trip, thanks. Is it somebody more advanced than we are," Archer contemplated, "trying to change the near past? Or are they in the far distant future? I'd like to ask T'Pol what she thinks. Do I dare?"

"I wouldn't," Tucker bluntly announced. "She's always enjoyed a rigid thought process. Today I think you shook her with your free-roaming methods. Throw time tampering into the mix? I'm scared enough for both her and me.

"Higher level physics break down rationality," Tucker continued. "Progress at that level comes from intuitive leaps, like Einstein imagining what it was like to ride a beam of light."

"No Vulcan would do that," Archer said. "It's not possible to ride a beam of light."

Tucker lowered his chin. "It is now."

Archer smiled. "They think emotionalism, unchecked, will destroy. It's made them afraid. But look at Hoshi. She's terrified every time something happens, but she keeps moving. She always moves to the next step, past the point of fear. Humans might go off in forty wrong directions, but the forty-first might take us someplace new."

Tucker contributed, "Vulcans never want to get off the trail."

"Well," he began instead, "you can sit inside and watch through the window while children play in the street, and say how they might get hurt out there. You can be the little old ladies of the galaxy, but you don't have any fun, and before long nobody talks to you. The Vulcans have wrapped it in a shell of elegance. If I told her that, what do you think she'd say?"

Tucker's face screwed up as he tried to pretend a Vulcan point of view. "Probably something about men in Earth history like Stalin and Li Quan—they were given the power to get anything they wanted, measured by their idea of 'fun.' "

"Good point. I think we agree it's dangerous for these beings from the future to help the Suliban, but it's not so different from an advanced race like the Vulcans coming and helping Earth. If it's so risky, why are they helping us at all? They didn't help the Klingons, did they?"

"No, nor anybody else, if I read the subtle side correctly. I've never heard a single Vulcan talk about any other race they shepherded."

Tucker laughed. "I'll ask her that one myself."

Archer nodded, agreeing with the sentiment but not the plan. "The idea of time travel itself is, on its face, illogical. Isn't it?"

"No," Tucker seized. "She'd have to agree with me on

this. The illogical doesn't exist in science. There is something we don't yet understand that allows time travel to take place."

Archer troubled to understand what Tucker had just said, and for a moment forgot about T'Pol. Instead, he found himself remembering Sarin. "If travel backward in time can take place, then causality doesn't exist. If causality doesn't exist, where is logic? 'A' plus 'B' causes 'C.' "

"But causality *does* take a beating at a level of quantum physics. It seems to break down at certain points. Are we discussing whether or not time travel is possible?" Tucker asked. "Or why anybody would be stupid enough to try it?"

"Both," Archer said. "First, is it possible, and second, why would anybody do it, because you can go back and destroy yourself very easily. If I go back and stop an Austrian farmer in the mid-1800s and ask him directions while he's on his way to the market, he gets to the market five minutes later, and misses meeting the woman he was supposed to marry. She passes by. Because they never met, Adolf Hitler is never born. World War II never happens, or happens later for other reasons, and the technological rush of the mid-20th century is delayed thirty or forty years . . . Zephram Cochrane doesn't have the infrastructure he needs to invent warp drive, and we never meet the Vulcans."

"Instead of meeting the Vulcans," Tucker picked up, "we meet the Klingons instead. By now, the Klingons are dominant on Earth and using Earth as a toehold in this whole section of the galaxy."

"A butterfly flaps its wings in Africa," Archer murmured, "and there's a typhoon in China the next spring.

This idea that anyone can engineer the future by screwing up the past—"

"John," Tucker interrupted, "could it be possible they *want* to screw up their own time? Are they insane, maybe?"

Archer didn't have the answer, but the question made him think of something else. "Or . . . are they reacting to something? Are these people from the future being forced to action, the way Vulcans and humans are forced to put weapons on our ships because there are hostile powers out there? Are they being forced to tamper with the past to stop somebody else from tampering?"

"Sure *seems* insane."

"I wish I could talk to these people for five minutes . . . if we have no way of knowing, how can we act?"

"With you laid up, there won't be any action. T'Pol—she'll just say since we have no basis on which to act, then you should do nothing."

"That's the difference between us," he reminded. "Since we have no basis, I'll act on what I *do* know. They took the Klingon, they have no right, and we're taking him back."

Archer bristled at his own conclusion and looked at Tucker for the support he knew would be there. This whole episode had been anything but proactive. Instead of making things happen, they had been involved in a scheme of making things *not* happen.

He wanted to change that.

"I just have one thing," Tucker slowly added. "What's the moral imperative to protect the future?"

"None," Archer said with a jolt of enthusiasm. "It hasn't happened yet."

The ship shuddered under them suddenly, cutting off the conversation.

"Captain . . ." Tucker made a tentative step toward the door.

"Sure, Trip, go mind your engines. Thanks for helping me work through this. If we know some questions, we'll have a way to recognize the answers when they come."

"I love the concrete! Call if you need me." Embracing that which he *could* control to some degree, Tucker was gone in a flash.

When he was alone, Archer looked out the window at the streaks of stars they were passing at remarkable new speeds. *We're here, Dad . . . warp four point five.*

He cleared his throat and touched the nearest computer link. "*Enterprise* starlog, Captain Jonathan Archer. April sixteenth, 2151 . . ."

Starlog.

"No, no—delete that. Begin recording . . . Captain's log, April sixteenth, 2151. We've been tracking the Suliban's ship for ten hours, thanks to our science officer, who came up with a way to tweak the sensors—computer, pause."

He let his head drop back and spoke aloud to the nearest sympathetic ear. "I save her life . . . and now she's helping us with the mission. One good turn deserves another? Doesn't sound very Vulcan."

He stopped mumbling, thought about what he had just said, what he and Tucker had talked about before, and about the future—all the different possible versions.

"Resume log."

The computer bleeped to assure him it was recording.

"I have no reason to believe Klaang is still alive. But, if the Suliban woman was telling the truth, it's crucial we try to find him. Computer . . . pause."

His back was aching in this position. He pulled Tucker's pillow out from under his leg and sat up. Sitting down just wasn't getting him in the right frame of mind. With care, he pushed off the chair again and put new pressure on his leg.

He moved across the room to where Porthos lay digesting a fine nonvegetarian meal. He scratched the dog's nose thoughtfully. "Have you ever known a Vulcan to return a favor? No, neither have I."

So he and Tucker were right—there was more going on with T'Pol than just guilt about his risking his own life to save hers. Officers, soldiers, shipmates did that for each other all the time. He couldn't believe selflessness was so new to Vulcans that they had only found it here. They'd been in space a long time, and you can't do that without a scaffold of cooperation and generosity toward each other, whether you admit it's there or not.

He scratched the dog and thought about his conversation with Tucker about time tampering. He wished he could discuss it with T'Pol, because he needed a cool head when it came to such long-range theoreticals, but all his internal alarms stopped him.

"Resume log. I still haven't decided whether to ask Sub-Commander T'Pol about this temporal cold war . . . my instincts tell me not to trust her—"

He paused. Something had just changed. The vibrations coming up through his injured leg were different from a few seconds ago.

He looked at the window. The stars were changing. The ship was falling out of warp!

"Computer, pause. Archer to T'Pol. Report!"

"If you're feeling well enough to come to the bridge, Captain," her voice called with a thread of tension, "now would be a good time."

CHAPTER 12

THE TEMPORAL ARCHWAY GLOWED AND SIZZLED AS IF IN anger. The barrier of energy blocking the way to the future, and also providing a window to it, now glared fitfully in its cylindrical housing. The murky, milky figure of the future being stood passively, but Silik could tell the individual was displeased.

"Did Sarin give them anything?" it asked.

"I don't know," Silik said, both truthful and impatient. He didn't like being made responsible for dangerous things of such undefinition.

"What do you know?" the figure demanded.

"They followed us here."

"Looking for Klaang? Or for you?"

"I don't know. But I'll destroy them before they locate the Helix."

The being was still for many seconds. When it spoke again, the words curdled Silik's blood to his very core.

"We didn't plan to involve the humans, or the Vulcans.

Not yet. Sarin's message cannot reach Qo'noS. If the humans have it, you must stop them."

"It's a gas giant."

Archer settled into his command chair as T'Pol stepped out of it, and eyed the big orange mass on the viewscreen—a gargantuan planet of mostly gravity and dust holding each other together on a vast scale.

"From the looks of it, a class six or seven," he muttered.

"Class seven," T'Pol confirmed. "The Suliban vessel dropped to impulse a few hours ago and altered course. Their new heading took them through its outer radiation belt."

"We've lost them?"

Reluctantly, she nodded.

"Move us in closer."

Mayweather glanced at him, then worked to obey that order. Archer pushed out of his chair and paced, working his leg to keep it from stiffening up. Phlox's pet liver had done a good job. He felt twinges, but no loss of strength.

The ship moved closer toward the radiation belt of the orange gas giant. The planet loomed large and imposing on their screens, causing warnings to go off on several stations, but not the right ones.

"Anything?" he asked.

"The radiation's dissipating their warp trail," Reed reported. "I'm only picking up fragments."

Archer gave T'Pol his hunting-eagle glare. "You finished helping us?" he challenged.

She went to Reed's station and eyed the graphics, then hit a control. One simple click.

On the main screen, an enhanced picture of the giant appeared, this time with a fragmented ion trail faintly traced in colors, being broken up by the winds.

"Lieutenant," she said, "run a spectral analysis of the fragments."

Reed hit a series of controls in specific order. On the graphic, a sequence of numbers appeared near each fragment, all different.

"There's too much distortion," Reed complained. "The decay rates don't even match."

"Calculate the trajectory of each fragment."

He looked a bit dubious, and glanced at Archer, who nodded. "You heard her."

Reed clearly hadn't a clue what she was looking for, but he did as he was bidden.

T'Pol, while Reed worked, turned and met Archer's eyes. For the first time they seemed to be thinking the same thing.

The graphic now displayed telemetry for each fragment. Archer nodded at T'Pol, who moved to another station and began doing the work for herself.

"Recalibrate the sensor array," Archer authorized. "Narrowband, short to midrange."

"Measure the particle density of the thermosphere," T'Pol added.

Archer looked at her again. "Those fragments weren't from the Suliban ship."

T'Pol confirmed, "They were from fourteen . . . and all within the last six hours. I believe we've found what we're looking for."

Despite her reticence until now, she had a lilt of victory in her voice.

Archer dropped a hand on Reed's shoulder. "How are your targeting scanners?"

"Aligned and ready, sir!"

"Bring weapons on-line and polarize the hull plating."

The crew jumped to action all over the bridge. That was no by-the-book order!

Armed conflict during the shakedown voyage!

"Lay in a sixty degree vector," Archer said calmly. "We're going in."

CHAPTER 13

EVERYONE WAS AT HIS STATION. THE APPEARANCE OF THEM there was beginning to gain a rhythm in the captain's mind. He had started knowing which person he was addressing without turning to see who was there. He felt their tension without any words to confirm it. He knew what they were feeling and sometimes thinking.

Intensity could do that.

The *Enterprise* moved through disruptions of gaseous energy and storms the size of whole planets. Her running lights cut through the dense layers, but it was still strangely similar to that ice cyclone on Rigel Ten.

Hoshi's little voice at his side had a new tremor in it when she spoke this time. "Sensor resolution's falling off at about twelve kilometers . . ."

Archer leaned forward. "Travis?"

Mayweather worked feverishly. "I'm okay, Captain."

The ship trembled and rolled—full swings her entire beam-width from side to side. Even her massive power was nothing against the natural monstrosity of a gas giant. This was a terrible risk, something Archer knew would take weeks of exploration, testing, and measurements in another circumstance.

He wanted to know what the ship could do. This would tell him.

T'Pol worked almost anxiously at her console. "Our situation should improve. We're about to break through the cyclohexane layer."

The orange color gave way to an even denser layer of roiling blue liquid. The blue color, normally peaceful, seemed even angrier than the outer atmosphere, and more eerie. It was also more solid, slamming the bow every few seconds with powerful strikes. The ship trembled so hard that Archer held himself in place with both hands.

"I wouldn't exactly call this an improvement," Archer commented.

"Liquid phosphorescence," T'Pol explained. "I wouldn't have expected that beneath a layer of cyclohexane."

The ship rocked sideways again, then took a hard drop forward.

Hoshi hunched her shoulders and hung on until her knuckles turned white. "You might think about recommending seat belts when we get home."

"It's just a little bad weather," Archer assured.

The roiling on the main screen thinned and changed again.

The console near Hoshi suddenly cried out—*peep peep peep peep!*

"We've got sensors!" she called at the same pitch.

"Level off," Archer ordered. "Go to long-range scan."

He almost corrected himself—long-range meant a light-year. This was just a planetary atmosphere. On a starship level, this was next door. But they seemed to understand his context.

"I'm detecting two vessels," T'Pol reported, "bearing one-one-nine mark 7."

"Put it up."

Hoshi worked her board. The viewscreen changed to show two Suliban ships moving away in the distance. The little vessels were unique to Archer's eyes, about twice the size of shuttlepods.

"Impulse and warp engines," Reed reported.

"What kind of weapons?" Archer asked.

"We're too far away."

"Sir," Mayweather broke in, "I'm picking up something at three-forty-two mark 12 . . . and it's a lot bigger!"

The viewscreen shifted as Hoshi worked faster.

"All sensors," Archer instructed T'Pol. "Get whatever you can!"

Before them on the changing screen, a huge complex came into focus. Was it a ship? Or buildings? Archer couldn't tell, but it was massive. It had to be free-floating, because this gas giant had no surface.

"Go tighter."

The screen zeroed in closer. The complex was indeed some kind of moving object, made of hundreds of Suliban ships interlocked to form a massive spiraled space station. A few individual cell ships engaged and disengaged from the mother complex.

"Biosigns?" he asked.

"Over three thousand," Hoshi reported. "but I can't isolate a Klingon, if there is one—"

A jolt rammed the body of the ship.

"That was a particle weapon, sir," Reed reported, too little and too late.

Hit again!

"Bridge!" a call came in from Trip Tucker. "We're taking damage down here! What's going on?"

"Just a little trouble with the bad guys," Archer assured. He used his voice as a tool, uttering pointless vocalizations just to show them he was in control and not ready to be afraid. Somehow the Suliban didn't scare him so much anymore. The fight with them on the planet had equalized things. T'Pol was wrong—the Suliban weren't so much more advanced than he was. Maybe the mystery had gone away, or maybe he was concentrating on the bigger badder guys from the future who could use such as the Suliban as a tool.

"I suggest returning to the phosphorous layer," T'Pol called over the *boom* of the next hit.

"Take us up," Archer obliged.

The ship rapidly ascended, leaving the attacking cell ships behind with admirable grace. The Suliban cells quickly homed toward the main complex.

Prodding, Archer asked a general question to any who wanted to contribute. "What've you got?"

"It appears," T'Pol began, "to be an aggregate structure, comprised of hundreds of vessels. They're held in place by an interlocking system of magnetic seals."

Not unheard of in the realm of shipbuilding and tactical considerations. Apartment buildings had been around for thousands of years, aircraft carriers and trains—there were plenty of examples of composite ships out there. Archer resolved not to be intimidated.

"There!" Hoshi yelped. "Right there!"

Biodata tumbled across the main screen over a small section of the Suliban aggregate.

"These bioreadings are not Suliban!" she added.

T'Pol looked at her. "We can't be certain they're Klingon," she warned.

"Even if it is Klaang," Archer accepted, "we'd have a tough time getting him off of there."

Reed turned in his chair and broached a touchy subject. "We could always try the transporting device. . . ."

"No," Archer quietly said. "We've risked too much to bring him back inside out. Would the grappler work in a liquid atmosphere?"

"I believe so . . ."

"Bring it on-line. One more time, Mr. Mayweather. Take us down to proximity range."

"Proximity range, sir."

Once again the ship descended into the smooth lower atmosphere, the clear layer that seemed so welcoming, yet held the primary threat.

"Make it aggressive," Archer said. "Don't hold back."

"Understood, sir," Mayweather agreed. "I won't."

The ship hummed with power, and soared like a giant albatross on an arctic crest.

"Suliban ships in patrol formation, sir," Reed instantly reported. "They've seen us!"

"Let's give them a closer look, Mr. Mayweather."

"Aye, sir!"

"Mr. Reed, open fire."

"Oh, thank you, sir, so much."

"Ready that grappling system."

"It shall indeed be ready, sir."

The ship took a compressive dive into the clear, burst

out, and trumpeted her presence in the sky. Rapid-blast torpedoes of compressed energy made a luminous announcement.

The artillery shells spoke out across the giant's sky-bound seas and scattered through the Suliban patrol. Were there hits? Archer couldn't tell. The Suliban returned fire, but also broke formation.

Enterprise absorbed a tremendous hit.

"The ventral plating's down!" Reed called over the noise. "I'm having trouble getting a weapons lock! These scanners weren't designed for a liquid atmosphere!" Again the ship was hit, driving him to comment, "Though apparently theirs were . . ."

A hard shake caused the console next to Hoshi to blow a plume of sparks. She shrieked and leapt back.

"Hold your position, Travis," Archer said calmly.

"The lead ship's closing," Reed reported. "Seven thousand meters . . . six thousand . . ."

"We should ascend!" T'Pol called.

"Hold your position!" Archer repeated. He didn't like repeating.

Reed glanced at him. "One thousand meters. Forward plating's off-line!"

"Now, Mr. Reed!"

One of the cell ships veered almost directly to the starship's bow. Reed struck his controls. Two grappling devices shot from ports on the launch bay arm, trailing thin cables that Archer could see partly on the forward screen.

The grapplers struck the Suliban ship and magnetically adhered to its hull. Archer gripped his chair, glad that metal was metal on any side of the galaxy.

"He's ejecting!" Hoshi called, and pointed.

A cockpit hatch sprang open on the Suliban cell. The pilot was gone in a blast of vapor and disappeared through the layer below.

To land where? Archer winced. No surface . . .

He hoped the Suliban had that covered, but there was no way to tell.

"Back up, Travis," he ordered.

"Rising, sir."

The ship moved back up toward the turbulent layers, now trailing its prey on a silken cord, drawing it closer and closer to the hangar bay.

Reed eyed his station and uttered, "Hello . . . their ship is in the launch bay, sir."

Archer nodded. Reed smiled. A new toy.

Fifteen minutes later, he and Mayweather and Tucker crowded around a table graphic in the situation room off the bridge. The table showed graphics of the cell ship, all different angles of the exterior, engine schematics, flight controls . . . they tried to study these while the starship trembled and shook around them, battling the turbulence, but she was built to do that, like ships immemorial before her.

"All right, what's this?" Mayweather was pointing at something.

"The pitch control," Tucker said. He sounded confident about that one.

"No," Mayweather argued. "*That's* the pitch control. This is the guidance system."

"Pitch control . . . guidance system . . . I got it."

"The docking interface," Mayweather went on. "How do you deploy it?"

Archer hunched over the graphics. "Looks like you release the inertial clamps here, here, and here, then initialize the coaxial ports."

"Good. Where's the auxiliary throttle?"

"Mmmm—" Tucker squinted. "It's not this one . . ."

Mayweather straightened up then. "With all due respect to Commander Tucker, I'm pretty sure I could fly this thing, sir."

"I don't doubt it," Archer agreed. "But I need you here."

"Captain?" T'Pol's voice thrummed under a low-frequency *boooom* that suddenly grew louder and erupted in a hard *bam.*

They turned.

"That charge contained a proximity sweep," she said from her post. "If we remain here, they're going to locate us."

Archer nodded and turned to Mayweather. "You're gonna have to speed this up a little, Travis."

"How complicated can it be?" Tucker howled. "Up, down, forward, reverse! We'll figure it out."

Booooom! Boooooom!

"Inverted depth charges, Captain!" T'Pol called.

She didn't have to report the damage. Archer could feel it. He stepped out to her, and she met him in the middle of the bridge. "We'll be back before you know it. Have Mayweather plot a course for Qo'noS."

"There's a Vulcan ship less than two days away," T'Pol offered. "It's illogical to attempt this alone."

"I was beginning to think you understood *why* we have to do this alone."

She paused. "You could both be killed."

He looked up, rather sharply. "Am I sensing concern? Last time I checked, that was considered an emotion."

As soon as he said it, he regretted his cocky accusation. She hadn't deserved that. Now who was the one doing the deliberate hurting and insulting?

T'Pol's expression turned blank again. "If anything happens to either of you, the Vulcan High Council will hold me responsible."

Archer smiled at her, offering a little understanding. Then Reed approached with two silver equipment cases, and Archer's attention went there. "You're finished?"

Reed flipped the lid on one case to reveal a rectangular device. "It should reverse the polarity of any maglock within a hundred meters. Once you've set the sequence, you'll have five seconds."

Archer looked down at the device with appreciation.

"One more thing," Reed added. He flipped open the second case and pulled out two Starfleet-colored hand weapons with pistol grips and handed them both to Archer.

"Ah—our new weapons?"

"They're called 'phase pistols,' " Reed introduced. "They have two settings. Stun and kill. It would be best not to confuse them."

Another low *boom* shook the vessel under them, followed by a startling jolt that rocked them back to the moment.

To T'Pol he said, almost with delight, "The ship is yours! Trip, let's go!"

CHAPTER 14

CRAMPED, TREMBLING, COLD, AND ADMITTEDLY OUT OF THEIR element, Jonathan Archer and Trip Tucker hunkered elbow to elbow inside the little Suliban cell ship as it blew free of the *Enterprise* and shot out into the swirling atmospheric sea. Visibility was almost nil—just a wall of blue gas.

Tucker gripped the controls with passionate terror and forced himself to concentrate almost yard by yard as the ship raced forward, fighting its own power and the turbulence at the same time.

Archer flinched when a light came on. "What's that?"

"Travis said not to worry about that panel."

"That's reassuring . . ."

They were thrown against each other when the cell hit an atmospheric pocket. Tucker held the steering mechanism with both hands and battled to compensate. He was dripping sweat despite the cold.

Queasy and bloodless, Archer fought to keep steady himself. "They sure didn't build these things for comfort."

"Wait till we get the Klingon in here with us. If I'm reading this right, we should be about twenty kilometers from *Enterprise.*"

"Drop the pitch thirty degrees."

"Look! The *Enterprise!*"

For just an instant, the visibility cleared, just enough to show a portion of the starship above them taking a hard whack from a luminous weapon stream.

"They're taking a lot of bad fire," Archer mentioned. "I should've given her permission for evasive maneuvers. If they change position, the Suliban'll have to look for them all over again."

"If they move, *we* might never find them again," Tucker reminded. "She'll probably just ride it out."

Archer gazed at the vision of the ship just as it disappeared again in a curtain of blue muck. He saw T'Pol's face, determined to hold position and give them their best shot, and he silently apologized to her for his snotty remarks. "That's what I'm counting on."

Tucker shouldered into a maneuver, his lips tight and his eyes squinting. "You've changed your tune about her. . . ."

"I think it's changing some," Archer agreed. "After a whole lifetime of watching Vulcans generalize about humans, seems I was doing the same thing about them. I just took it out on her." He found a sheepish little grin and bounced it off Tucker. "I think I'll stop now."

Tucker's expression was dubious, but accepting of the redesigned attitude. Even hopeful?

"Look at this," he said then, pointing at the adjusting screens. "I think we're there."

"Bring the docking interface on-line."

Tucker went for a button—then stopped. He chose a

completely different button. The interface hummed to life. The cell ship rattled around them.

"Coaxial ports," Archer ordered.

Another control twanged. A quick, hissing sound blew some kind of ballast or docking mechanisms somewhere on the skin of the cell ship. Tucker embraced the steering mechanism and began to ease the ship downward. Through the ports, they could see blue phosphorous clouds begin to thin out. A moment later, they broke into clear space.

"Where is it?" Tucker gulped. "It was right there!"

Squinting through a sheet of sweat, Archer studied the graphic. "Bank starboard ninety degrees."

Tucker heaved the controller over. The ship banked sharply, taking their stomachs with it.

A dizzying view of the Suliban complex rose directly below them.

"There you are!" Tucker howled.

"That's the upper support radius," Archer said, proud that he could recognize anything in that mass. "Drop down right below it. Start a counterclockwise sweep."

The cell ship descended further, down past numerous levels of the aggregate. Other cell ships, most larger, engaged and disengaged from the huge structure for reasons of their own. Tucker slowed their descent just in time. He was getting the hang of maneuvering this contraption. Archer didn't make any distracting comments, but did help judge distances.

"A little more . . . little more . . . almost there . . ."

Scrrrape.

Again they were thrown against each other. Archer

shot him a look as they both got a touch of nostalgia about their inspection tour—how many days ago now?

"Right here," Archer said. "All stop."

The cell bonked to a halt. Through the port, they could see a circular airlock protruding from the Suliban complex. Tucker looked at him. Archer nodded. Why not?

They both began manipulating the controls. The ship began moving horizontally now, through the airlock.

Chhhh-UNK.

Contact. The cell jolted slightly. A series of whirring mechanical sounds signaled that the docking ports were locking into place. They knew those sounds. Everybody who flew knew those sounds.

Abruptly, the hatch opened—on its own!

Archer flinched and put his hand on Tucker's arm. Before them was a long, dimly lit corridor, completely unoccupied. Their own private entrance.

Tucker looked at him. "Well?"

Archer pulled out his phase pistol. "Why not?"

With their weapons drawn, they moved quickly through the corridor. Tucker carried the silver case with the magnetic disruption device inside. Archer kept eyeing the sensor scanner he held in his other hand. They rounded a corner, and came face to face with a—a face!

Caught by surprise, the Suliban soldier clutched for his own side arm, but Archer fired first.

The soldier dropped like a bag of sand.

For a moment, Archer and Tucker stood over him and looked at the weapon in Archer's hand. Nice little unit.

"Stun seems to work . . ." he commented.

And they kept moving.

Enterprise

"Anything?"

T'Pol's question provided mostly irritation to the crew around her.

Lieutenant Reed had nothing to report, but simply gripped his console as they rode out the nasty bit of weather and artillery fire. Beside him, Hoshi Sato had her earpiece tightly wedged in.

"The phosphorous is distorting all the EM bands," she said dubiously—then she yanked her earpiece out and called, "Grab onto something!"

Two rapid *booms* throbbed through the skin of the ship, followed immediately by two sharp jolts powerful enough to send the whole ship on a dive. Reed flinched as the console before him blew out, lathering his face with sparks. Streams of gas and showers of debris doused the bridge.

Reed pulled himself back to the console as the sparking reduced itself automatically. Was anyone hurt? He glanced around—no, Mayweather seemed all right. So did Hoshi, though shaken. T'Pol still held the command chair, and gave no orders to break off their course or altitude.

"This is ridiculous!" Reed complained. "If we don't move the ship, Captain Archer won't have anything to look for when he gets back!"

T'Pol had a stubborn streak, but she wasn't foolish. After a moment of consideration, she turned to Hoshi. "We're going to need that ear of yours."

Hoshi pulled herself back to her position and pressed the listening device to her ear again.

"Mr. Mayweather," T'Pol addressed, "move us away, five kilometers."

"In what direction?"

"Any direction."

The ship trembled with effort, and began to rise. Malcolm Reed held his breath, knew this was his suggestion, and although he also knew everyone else was thinking the same thing, he began now a whole new worry.

Though they would now survive to be found, how would the captain and Tucker find them?

Klingon life-signs. A whole new quiver for an Earth sensor system.

However, being a machine, the sensor didn't care one way or the other and led them dutifully to the source.

Archer went through the door first, with Tucker right behind him, weapons drawn. And there was their big buddy, restrained in an elaborate chair-like thing, with tubes and devices attached to his body. He was alive, but semiconscious. Through a window, steel-blue light flowed from the phosphorous layer, lending a weird cast to the Klingon's skin, and Archer's and Tucker's, too.

Archer gestured. Tucker immediately went to the Klingon and started unstrapping him. The Klingon stared, but didn't fight or make any noise.

"This is gonna be easier than I thought," Tucker said winningly. "It's okay," he added to Klaang. "We're getting you off this thing."

The third and final restraint slapped to the floor. Klaang, now free, suddenly erupted. He raised his arm, clubbed Tucker in the chest, and very easily blew the engineer across the room. Tucker landed in a heap, shocked. Klaang stood to his full height and ripped the tubes and wires from his limbs.

Locking his stance, Archer raised his weapon—the interstellar common language.

"I really don't want to have to carry you out of here," he warned.

Klaang grew much more passive in the face of the unfriendly weapon. He wisely hesitated.

"I think he gets the idea," Archer said. "Give him a hand."

Tucker hesitated, too, not wanting to get close to the enormity again, but he steeled himself and gave Klaang a supporting hand as they followed Archer out the door.

Bearing the weight of the huge Klingon, Tucker rapidly became a gasping lump following Archer through the corridor.

"Qu'taw boh!" the Klingon roared, half dazed.

"Be quiet," Archer snapped.

"Muh tok!"

A blast tore a chunk out of the wall. Suliban soldiers!

Archer dove to the left, Tucker and Klaang to the right, for cover.

"Dajvo Tagh! Borat!"

"You tell him, big guy." Tucker hid behind the Klingon—or was he pinned back there?

"Give me the box," Archer called.

Trip slid the silver case's strap off his shoulder and handed it to him. Just then, a Suliban attacker rushed into view from an adjoining corridor and caught them by surprise. As the Suliban took aim at Archer and Tucker, the Klingon suddenly rose like a grizzly bear.

The Suliban was caught under its chin and went flying into a bulkhead. Klaang followed him, caught him, and joyously pounded him unconscious.

A moment later he simply turned and came back to Archer and Tucker, rumbling with satisfaction.

"Thanks," Tucker said—more of that interstellar language.

But their moment of unity was ruined by another Suliban, and another after him, and more weapons blasting at them.

"Get to the ship!" Archer ordered. "I'll be right behind you!"

Tucker shot him a horrified look, but he had agreed not to argue. Getting the Klingon off was the important thing. Tucker grabbed the mountainous stranger and hauled him down the corridor.

Archer crouched, alone now, with the silver case. He removed the rectangular device and attached it with its own magnetics to the nearest wall, then activated it with the encoded authorization.

Then he dropped to his knees and covered his head, and hoped to live.

CHAPTER 15

A LOW-PITCHED WHINE DEAFENED ARCHER AS HE HUDDLED too near the magnetic damper. Only two seconds passed before the device emitted a blinding pulse of energy that radiated in all directions.

Archer was blown over onto his side. As the light receded, he struggled to his feet and found all his arms and legs still with him. The corridor was trembling, shuddering! Thousands of magnetic docking ports unlocking—

The floor began to separate under his feet—the entire corridor was splitting in two! Force fields flashed on as the interlocking elements making up this section of the aggregate lost their cohesion. He was cut off.

He had no choice but to turn and run in the other direction, and hope Tucker and Klaang got through.

The entire upper section of the Suliban aggregate was dismantling over Archer's head. He imagined the huge sections, comprised of dozens of cell ships, disengaging from the central mass, tumbling away into the blue atmosphere, powerless and pilotless.

"Captain? Captain!" Tucker's voice called at him under the *boom* and *clack* of disengagement.

Archer found a corner to duck behind and clawed for his communicator. "It worked," he said without formality.

"Where are you?"

"I'm still in the central core. Get Klaang back to *Enterprise.*"

"What about you, sir?"

"Get him back to the ship! You can come back for me."

Lies, all lies.

"It's going to be hard to isolate your biosigns," Tucker protested. "So stay as far away from the Suliban as you can."

Archer breathed a gush of relief that Tucker intended to follow the very hard order to leave someone behind. Nobody liked that one. Nobody ever wanted to do it the first time out.

"Believe me," he vowed, "I'll try."

Inside the Suliban cell ship, Trip Tucker gritted his teeth against leaving John Archer on that floating junkheap. Beside him, crammed in like a sausage in its skin, the Klingon spat and coughed protests about the accommodations.

"RaQpo jadICH!"

"I don't particularly like the way you smell, either," Tucker opined.

"MajQa!"

Tucker ignored the comment and kept sweeping for the *Enterprise.*

"I don't get it . . . this is right where they're supposed to be."

He adjusted his scanners, hoping the alien contraption was just plain wrong.

It wasn't. There was no one out there. Nothing.

"The charges are getting closer again."

Malcolm Reed tugged at the collar of his uniform tunic as the fifth low-frequency *boom* in as many seconds rolled over the starship.

"Another five kilometers, Ensign," T'Pol ordered.

Mayweather worked the controls on the helm. "At this rate, the captain'll never find us."

"Wait a minute!" Hoshi interrupted. "I think I've got something!"

"Amplify it!" T'Pol ordered with endearing passion.

Hoshi tapped her controls. A cacophony of noises, radio signals, background noise, and distortion blasted through the bridge.

"It's Commander Tucker!"

How had she deciphered that from these crackles?

"All I hear is noise," Reed pointed out.

"Sshhh! Listen . . . it's just a narrow notch in the midrange . . . he says he's about to ignite his thruster exhaust!"

T'Pol moved quickly to her viewing hood and peered inside. "Coordinates—one fifty-eight mark . . . one three."

"Laid in!" Mayweather confirmed.

"Ahead, fifty kph." She turned to Hoshi, and for the first time regarded the other woman with respect. *"Shaya tonat."*

Hoshi offered a small smile. "You're welcome."

They all watched the sensors, though they could see very little on any screen that wasn't the shifting of atmospheric chaos.

"Two kilometers, dead ahead," Mayweather said, carefully maneuvering the ship to avoid a deadly collision—deadly for the Suliban pod that held their shipmates.

"Initiate docking procedures." T'Pol authorized.

Hoshi turned to them, her face gray. "I'm only picking up two biosigns . . . one Klingon . . . one human."

Somehow, a hunted animal knows, senses, that it's being hunted. Jonathan Archer felt like a rabbit in a fox's den. He clung to the help of his little scanning device, which showed two Suliban moving away from a central indicator. They'd lost him.

But he was far from out of trouble. He squatted behind a metal beam more than eight feet off the deck. When he was sure he could jump down safely, without being heard, he did.

His leg, which until now had pretended to be completely healed, nearly buckled. He fell against the wall and steadied himself for a few seconds, and used those seconds to tap the scanner and give himself a wider view of the vicinity. Other blips showed still more Suliban, but there was a large area to one side with no life-signs at all.

Sanctuary. If he could get there, he might be able to hide for . . . long enough.

He made sure he wasn't going to collapse on that leg and hurried down the corridor.

When he found the pass to the empty area, the narrow passage looked completely different from anything he'd seen here before. It ended at a single door. Archer hesitated. Was he being herded? Funneled? He got that feeling. This area was too empty. Had he been lured here with a sense of safety?

Suddenly he felt vulnerable and somewhat foolish. On the other hand, he had nowhere else to go. Maybe there were still answers to be found here. He owed himself those answers, and he was beginning to realize that he owed them to T'Pol, to Admiral Forrest, and even to Soval and the Vulcans. He owed them a good, solid representation that humans and Vulcans *could* work together—yes, they could.

We can.

His vulnerability went away. If there was someone here who knew what was going on, Archer very much wanted a confrontation. As he closed in on the single door, his fears for himself dissolved. Escape went away as his primary objective.

The scanner's information was now heavily distorted. Why would it be?

As he approached the door, it opened for him. That alone confirmed his suspicion that someone was inviting him here.

He cautiously stepped through, expecting for a moment to be assaulted, but that didn't make sense. He could easily have been a sitting duck in the closed corridor.

Inside was some kind of vestibule—a passage without an exit.

He raised his arm—it stayed up after he put it down. . . . Lights distorted his vision . . . time began to slow . . . to slow . . .

Was he underwater? His movements slowed further. Time effect!

This was some kind of temporal alteration chamber. And Archer had walked right into it. His arms and legs blurred as he moved. Gradually, deliberately, he learned to make forward progress, to ignore the echoes he saw, movement echoes that unnerved him and confused his eyes. He moved his arms, and a second set made the same movement seconds later—or seconds before?

He looked down. The sound of his footsteps preceded the actual steps. He stopped walking. Soon he had only two feet again. When he had a little control—although his heartbeat had other ideas—he clapped his hands.

The sound came before his hands met.

Now what?

Definitely time distortion, contained somehow. Could he trust his own thoughts?

Moving with great deliberation, he began to explore the room, the alien architecture, the technology on undecipherable panels. After all, someone wanted him to see all this. He would oblige them.

A podium rose before him. As it did, as he was able to focus on it, the temporal distortions began to fade. Had someone been giving him a taste of what they could do, and now they were finished showing off? Had it been a test? A mistake?

There was the podium, clear now before him, and a large weird-looking archway—metallic, huge, obviously purposeful in design and whatever its function was. Certainly not just interior decor.

He drew his pistol and turned sharply when a reverberation rang through the chamber—the door was opening. Beyond it, the dark vestibule appeared empty. The door closed and sealed again, as if a ghost had entered . . . or left.

Archer backed away, silent, listening. His senses chimed with intuition.

"You're wasting your time. Klaang knows nothing."

A voice! Real words. What a relief—more or less.

The sound of footsteps in the preecho chamber rumbled with strange sounds and repeats. Archer tried to track the sound with his pistol, ready to shoot. The voice preechoed, too. He heard two, three, four of each word.

"It would be unwise to discharge that weapon in this room," the voice said.

"What is this room?" Archer asked. "What goes on here?"

"You're very curious, Jonathan. May I call you Jonathan?"

"Am I supposed to be impressed that you know my name?" he asked reasonably.

"I've learned a great deal about you. Even more than you know."

"Well, I guess you have me at a disadvantage," Archer said, leading this person on. He knew by now that whoever was talking desperately wanted to tell him many things, or he/it wouldn't be talking at all. "So why don't you drop the invisible man routine and let me see who I'm talking to?"

Because you know you're going to show me eventually.

"You wouldn't have come looking for Klaang," the voice said, "if Sarin had told you what she knew. That means you're no threat to me, Jonathan. But I do need you to leave this room."

The time-door hissed again, and opened invitingly.

"Now, please."

The footsteps echoed again, but this time Archer saw something, a slight distortion against the far wall.

Instead of leaving, he fired his phase pistol. A blurred preshot flowed in before the blast itself, and the sound had no attachment to what he saw. The beam struck the far wall. A jagged wave of energy blew from the point of impact and swept the room. Archer was blown back, slamming his head against a wall. Pain drummed in his skull—he held his head and waited for the wave to pass. It passed four times.

"I warned you not to fire the weapon," the voice said.

Again the distortion moved across the room.

Archer gasped, tried to steady his breathing, then spoke. "This chameleon thing . . . pretty fancy. Was it payment for pitting the Klingons against each other? A trophy from your temporal cold war?"

An embittered action blew across the room, ultrafast, and slammed Archer again against the wall. But this was different from the weapon shot. This one had pure anger in it. He'd made the intruder angry.

His pistol! His hand was empty! He grabbed around, but the weapon was gone.

Before him was a Suliban, now normalized against the background, its dappled face and skull still looking vaguely unreal. It held his pistol on him. As he stood with his eyes locked on those alien eyes, he recognized this as the leader of the attackers back at the spaceport on Rigel Ten. Not exactly a big surprise, and in a way, its own kind of win. Now he knew who he was up against, if not why.

"I was going to let you go," the Suliban said.

"Really?" Archer backed away slowly, trying to remember the timing of those echoes. "Then you obviously don't know as much about me as you thought you did."

"On the contrary," the Suliban said, "I could've told

you the day you were going to die. But I suppose that's about to change."

The Suliban opened fire on him with his own phase pistol.

The preecho struck Archer in the chest and drove him back. He brought up every muscle he could control and darted sideways before the actual bolt could strike him. Instead, it missed by an inch and burrowed into the wall. Archer spun behind a bank of alien consoles as the shock wave swept the room, knocking the Suliban down completely.

Archer was ready for that shock and braced against it. "What's the matter?" he chided. "No genetic tricks to keep you from getting knocked on your butt?"

"What you call tricks, we call progress!" the Suliban declared. "Are you aware that your genome is almost identical to that of an ape? The Suliban don't share humanity's patience with natural selection!"

"So, to speed things up a little, you struck a deal with the devil."

Archer was careful to hide. Assault might work against him. The Suliban's confusion in this echo chamber could be a weapon in itself, for, as advanced as the Suliban thought he was, Archer was able to adjust to this place. He was getting used to it. As he spoke, he positioned himself between the Suliban leader and the open timelock. Moving behind the consoles, he slowly removed the communicator from his belt. Carefully, he calculated the next trajectory of the temporal wave, then threw the communicator against a monitor on the far wall.

The monitor sparked. The preecho effect made a dozen communicators sail through the air, drawing the

Suliban's attention. The Suliban, disoriented, aimed clumsily and fired at the sparking monitor.

The shock wave thundered outward from the strike zone. The Suliban tried to brace himself against it this time, and managed to stay on his feet. But Archer had situated himself in the perfect spot to be thrown into the open time-lock vestibule.

He tumbled like a snowball through the door. The door began to close.

At the last moment, the intelligent and obviously strong-willed Suliban plunged toward the door and slipped through. The temporal compression began as the door locked and sealed itself.

Archer was locked in this small place, a place where time was in convulsions, with a Suliban whose plans he had wrecked. Each of them battled to be the first to gain control of his body.

The Suliban was raising the weapon again. . . .

Summoning every ounce of muscle control and sheer will, Archer shoved himself off the wall behind him and smashed into the Suliban in this eerie slow-motion chamber. The pistol jarred against his shoulder, dislodged from the Suliban's hand, and tumbled toward the floor. It struck the deck just as time returned to something like normal, and the fight was on.

Archer realized quickly he was no match for combat with an enhanced alien. He had to get the pistol!

Twisting viciously, he managed to pin the Suliban to the floor and lean on his opponent's wrists. It seemed to work, until the Suliban dislocated his own shoulder and wrist in a grotesque rotation and found a way to reach for the pistol, and got it. Archer certainly couldn't use human moves against something like this—so he punched the Suliban in the nose. That had to work all over the galaxy.

It did. The Suliban writhed and went momentarily limp. Archer shoved off him and bolted to the door.

The Suliban had the weapon.

Archer ran for his life. He hadn't intended for ass-n-elbows to be his plan, or the great final moments he ever had in mind for himself, but there was method in his madness—if he could keep the stubborn Suliban chasing him, then the *Enterprise* would have a chance to get away. A few minutes here, a few there . . . if Trip Tucker or Reed were in command, this would never work. He had left T'Pol in charge.

A Vulcan—the bane of his life—was going to make sure his plan was fulfilled. T'Pol would stick to her line of demarcation and do the logical thing. She would know there was no way for him to be found in this maze, no way for them to infiltrate, to risk a half dozen lives on a rescue mission into the guts of this aggregate, which was breaking up. She would make all the right arguments, shout Trip down, over-British Reed, deal with Hoshi's shrieks of protest, and she would finally seize the command Archer himself had confirmed. She would take the ship out of this mess, and Klaang, and she would succeed.

Not a bad legacy, Dad, for you or for me.

So he ran harder, taking the ache in his leg as validation of his personal honor. Behind him, the Suliban was coming out of the time-lock, aiming, firing—

CHAPTER 16

"OUR MISSION IS TO RETURN THE KLINGON TO HIS HOME-world. Another rescue attempt could jeopardize that mission—"

"The captain specifically told us to come back for him!"

"As commanding officer, it's *my* job to interpret the captain's orders."

Trip Tucker's anger flushed right up into his face and out the top of his head. "I just told you his orders! What's there to 'interpret'!"

Everyone on the bridge watched tensely as Tucker confronted T'Pol with his report and watched it pulled apart, brick by brick, and the captain with it.

T'Pol contained herself with damnable reserve. "Captain Archer may very well have told you to return for him later because he knew how stubborn you can be."

"What's that supposed to mean?"

"You might've risked Klaang's life in a foolish attempt to swing back and rescue the captain."

Tucker grimaced. "I can't believe this!"

A jolt from outside rocked the ship and punctuated his fury as the tension rose for them all. Reed was standing behind him, but said nothing. Hoshi looked positively destroyed at T'Pol's refusal. Mayweather's hands on the helm were stiff and flushed.

"The situation must be analyzed logically," T'Pol said, but this time it sounded like she was trying to convince herself as much as them.

"I don't remember the captain analyzing anything when he went back for you on that roof!" Tucker roared.

"That's a specious analogy."

"Is it?"

"We have work to do. We must stabilize our flight condition before we can move out of the atmosphere. Take your posts, please. That was not a request."

Well, she might not be Starfleet, but she had the style down. Everyone responded, though with a bitter silence. Tucker ground his teeth and went to the engineering master control station. What could he do? Was there a way to neutralize her command status?

"Hull plating's been repolarized," Reed reported. His voice was hardly more than a rasp. Behind it was the question in everyone's mind. *Leave the captain? Would he leave us?*

"Stand by the impulse engines. Mr. Tucker, status?"

Tucker felt a vicious tone rise from his throat. He thought about lying, stalling. But, ultimately, he couldn't do it. "The autosequencer's on-line, but annular confinement's still off by two microns."

"That should suffice," T'Pol said.

"Easy for you to say."

"If the Suliban have reestablished their defense, we'll have no other option."

The ship roared through the gas giant's atmosphere directly below the roiling blue layer. Several cell ships appeared on the scanners and began an attack pattern, strafing the underside of the huge dove-gray vessel. Reed, still under his fire-at-will order, took out his frustration with T'Pol on the incoming assault vessels.

"We have four more coming up off starboard!" he called.

T'Pol paused. "Can we dock, Ensign?"

Mayweather blinked. "These aren't ideal conditions—"

"Mr. Tucker, we're going to plan B."

Tucker swung around. What had changed her mind? Why would a person who claimed to be ruled by logic suddenly whip around to a completely crazy plan of action?

Who cared!

"I'm on my way!" he declared, and rushed off the bridge.

It was crazy, and he embraced it with everything he had. In less than two minutes he was in the newly installed transport-materializing chamber, summoning power from deep in the bowels of the ship's impulse drive system. Yes, crazy—he might find himself standing over the shredded, gurgling remains—

No, don't think that way. The control station fell under his trembling hands. Just work the controls . . . make the numbers line up . . . focus the beams . . .

"I'll do it," he murmured. "I'll do it, I can do it—"

He only had seconds. He felt the presence of T'Pol and Reed and all the others, even though they were decks away from him. This was it. T'Pol would never give him another chance. There was no plan C.

The chamber began to whine a god-awful noise. He

focused and focused, adjusted and hoped. If only Porthos were here, he could cross his paws.

A column of light appeared inside the chamber, between the two pie plates on floor and ceiling that would act as a receiver. Human readings . . . he was sure those were human readings. There was only one human on that big Suliban knot out there!

A humanoid shape appeared, forming between the lights. But the Suliban were humanoid. Tucker held his breath.

There was nothing more he could do with the controls. They would either do what they were designed to do, or there would be a disaster here.

The captain's build—the captain's hair and hands—a crouched position. Running?

Long seconds finally pulled Jonathan Archer together out of a puzzle of lights and whines. He stumbled forward on sheer momentum, then skidded and stopped himself, and looked around in shock at his new surroundings. He wavered, disoriented, then patted himself to see if he was all there.

"Bridge!" Trip called. "We've got him!" He rushed to the pad platform and reached for Archer. "Sorry, Captain! We had no other choice!"

Well, that was a silly thing to say, because there were always other choices, but at least it sounded better than anything else he could think of.

Archer stumbled down with Tucker's help.

"Are you hurt? Are you all here?"

"Well, I think so, most of me, anyway." Archer offered him a tremulous smile and a grip on the arm to prove to them both that they were together again.

"T'Pol wanted to leave you behind!"

Archer steadied himself with a hand on Tucker's shoulder. "She *wanted* to. Notice she didn't act on what she wanted. She acted on what she *could* do." He drew a breath of life and actually laughed. "Trip, old man, I believe I can work with that!"

CHAPTER 17

The Planet Qo'noS

THE GNARLED TOWERS OF THE KLINGON HIGH COUNCIL chamber rose above a smoggy yellow haze in the capital city. Inside the chambers, an ancient room of stone and wooden beams was hung with ceremonial banners and echoes of conquests stemming back through the pages of alien time. Guards stood everywhere, more for show than function, dressed in regalia and armed with archaic weapons. The Council members, seated at a serpentine table, pounded and shouted in their idea of debate.

There was great strife here today.

Jonathan Archer presented a calm demeanor, hoping his colleagues would take his cue in this shockingly alien environment. Alien, yes, but there was something hauntingly medieval about this place and these people, not really so far out of the human realm of imagination. Perhaps that was the disturbing part—the fact that they could empathize with being Klingon.

In a noble queue, Archer, T'Pol, and Hoshi moved into the enormous chamber, led by Klaang, who was so calm now as to be arguably majestic. Klaang was clearly working at both strength and dignity, despite what he had suffered physically.

He stopped before the Chancellor. *"Wo'migh Qagh! Q'apla!"*

Hoshi leaned toward Archer and whispered, "Something about disgracing the Empire . . . he says he's ready to die."

Archer murmured, "That's all we get out of this?"

The Chancellor was on his feet now, glaring in open curiosity at the humans. The wide-shouldered leader walked down the great stone steps, and as he did this, he drew a jagged dagger from its sheath.

Klaang tensed but never flinched as the Chancellor stopped in front of him.

Archer tensed also. If this thing were carried out, he would be helpless to stop it. At least he would show them that humans weren't squeamish and would stand up beside Klaang to the last. They hadn't brought him here just to be arbitrarily killed. The Chancellor would be forced to think about what he was doing, rather than just act by rote.

The Chancellor snatched Klaang's wrist and drew the blade across the palm, drawing blood. Archer winced and put his hand out slightly to his side to keep Hoshi steady. T'Pol remained unfazed.

"Poq!" the Chancellor called.

An aide approached with a vial, held it up, and caught several drops of Klaang's blood, while Klaang stood there, completely dumbfounded by all this.

The aide hurried to a large apparatus that remained undefined until he opened it and inserted the vial into a sensor padd. A large screen came to life suddenly, displaying a highly magnified cluster of lavender blood cells.

The Council members grumbled with sounds that might have been approval.

The image continued to enlarge, and became spirals of DNA. The spirals became larger and larger, until a distinctive pattern showed itself even to the untrained eye. The aide kept working the controls until individual molecules rose before the audience.

Hoshi drew a breath to speak, but Archer motioned her silent.

The molecular pattern began to rotate, revealing . . . what were those? Maps!

Maps, and text! Alien script written on a molecular level!

"Phlox should see this," Archer murmured. "He'd have a kitten."

Text, schedules, coordinates . . .

The entire chamber erupted in a rumble of approval. Then the Chancellor, purple-faced with excitement, stalked over to Archer.

He lifted the dagger to Archer's throat. Archer remained steady, but it took some doing.

"ChugDah hegh . . . volcha vay."

Just like that, the Chancellor lowered the weapon and stalked away.

Archer let himself breathe again. "I'll take that as a thank you. . . ."

Beside him, Hoshi offered, "I don't think they have a word for thank you."

"Then what'd he say?"

"You don't want to know."

The Klingon chamber began to shuffle with activity as the meeting broke up and the Council adored its DNA treasure. Now they could move on with whatever internal conflicts they had with their neighbors, the Suliban, or they could use the contraband information to get the Suliban to leave them alone. At least they knew now that their internal structure was being tampered with. They wouldn't turn against each other now. At least, not for a while.

Archer was willing to wait it out. Able to breathe normally for the first time in days, he turned and motioned his crew toward the door. "Ladies? Allow me to escort you to a much better place. We've done all we can here. Anybody got a silver bullet?"

CHAPTER 18

JONATHAN ARCHER STOOD UP AS THE DOOR CHIME ON HIS ready room jingled. "Come in."

T'Pol and Tucker came in, oddly side by side and not even spitting. What had gone on here while he was incommunicado?

"I've just gotten a response to the message I sent to Admiral Forrest," he told them. "He enjoyed telling the Vulcan High Command about the Suliban we ran into. It's not every day *he* gets to be the one dispensing information."

T'Pol looked quizzical, but she got the inference. Archer grinned and decided he owed Forrest an apology. The admiral had proven more canny than Archer had given him credit for. They now had a formally logged record of humans and Vulcans working together under duress, with two completely different methods of command—and doing all right together. Starfleet could do worse. It gave them all a platform from which to spring.

"I wanted you both to hear Starfleet's new orders before I inform the crew."

"Orders?" Tucker asked.

Archer nodded and looked at T'Pol. "Your people are sending a transport to pick you up."

She seemed hesitant, but buried it. "I was under the impression that *Enterprise* would be taking me back to Earth."

"It would be a little out of our way. Admiral Forrest sees no reason why we shouldn't keep going."

Tucker went up on his toes. "Son of a bitch!"

Archer smiled and agreed, "I have a feeling Dr. Phlox won't mind staying around for a while. He's developing a fondness for the human endocrine system."

"I'll get double watches on the repair work!"

"I think the outer hull's going to need a little patching up," Archer said. "Let's hope that's the last time somebody takes a shot at us."

"Let's hope!"

Oh, well, famous last words. *We'll see.*

Tucker, now very happy, spun on a heel and headed for the door. T'Pol started to follow him, but Archer stopped her.

"Would you stick around for a minute?" he asked.

She glanced at Tucker as the door shut between them, but turned again to the captain.

"Ever since I can remember," he began, "I've seen Vulcans as an obstacle, always keeping us from standing on our own two feet."

"I understand," she said quietly.

"No, I don't think you do. If I'm going to pull this off, there are a few things I have to leave behind. Things like preconceptions . . . holding grudges . . ." He paused, and tilted his head to soften his meaning. "This mission would've failed without your help."

"I won't dispute that," she said.

A retort popped up behind Archer's tongue, but he bit it off. Maybe she was joking. "I was thinking a Vulcan science officer could come in handy . . . but if I ask you to stay, it might look like I wasn't ready to do this on my own."

She raised her chin in that way she had. "Perhaps you should add pride to your list."

"Perhaps I should."

She considered his honesty, then said, "It might be best if I were to contact my superiors and make the request myself. With your permission," she added decorously.

Finally they understood each other. It felt good to be on the same page.

Archer smiled again. "Permission granted."

They stood together in companionable unity for a few moments as the ship streaked along at its new high-warp cruising speed.

"Will you join me on the bridge, Sub-Commander?" he asked, and gestured toward the door. "We have some good news for the crew, don't we?"

"Captain," she said with a lilt, "I will be honored to assist."

The other crew members were at their stations as he and T'Pol came out of the ready room. They might have suspected something was going on, but they seemed to be assuming the worst. Reed was straight as a stick. Mayweather was leaning forward on his helm controls, almost sagging. Hoshi's eyebrows were both up in anticipation. Tucker's absence bothered Archer a little, but he knew the engineer was larking about belowdecks, doing what he liked to do.

Archer came to a place on the bridge where he could see them all, and they could all see him. T'Pol politely moved a little off to one side and let him have the stage.

"I hope nobody's in a big hurry to get home," he began. "Starfleet seems to think we're ready to begin our mission. Mr. Reed, I understand there is an inhabited planet a few light-years from here?"

"Sensors show a nitrogen-sulfide atmosphere," Reed said, not exactly confirming or dismissing what Archer had just said.

"Probably not humanoids," Hoshi clarified.

"That's what we're here to find out," Archer reminded. "Travis, prepare to break orbit and lay in a course."

Mayweather looked up at him, beaming. "I'm reading an ion storm on that trajectory, sir . . . should I go around it?"

Archer smiled at him, at all of them, and turned to look at the swirl of open space, all the oxtails and elephant trunks, nebulae and anomalies out there to be gone through, and he brushed his toe on the deck of the ship that would take them there.

"We can't be afraid of the wind, Ensign," he said. "Take us to warp four."

BEHIND THE SCENES OF *ENTERPRISE*

Paul Ruditis

Concept

"Take her out . . . straight and steady."

"SOMEBODY ONCE SAID THAT THE TWO THINGS THAT FIRST started the Internet," explains Rick Berman, co-creator and executive producer of *Enterprise,* "were pornography and *Star Trek.*"

Rick Berman isn't making a joke.

After working for two and a half years developing the idea for the fifth television installment of the entertainment monolith known as *Star Trek,* he has heard any number of rumors detailing exactly what the series is going to be. From a Starfleet Academy show, to a series about a futuristic special-missions force, to a look at the future from the Klingon point of view, all sorts of ideas have been bandied about the Internet detailing what the fans *know* the production team is working on.

"Fans discussing the past, present, and future of *Star Trek* is something that has gone on forever," Berman admits. "We are conscious of it. We are respectful of it. We have people who are in touch with it and who keep us abreast of what the feelings of the fans are. But we have to eventually do what we think is best. That's not to say that some of the things that we hear don't influence us to some degree, but we can't let the fans create the show."

No matter what the rumors flying around fandom were, they all seemed to share a basic feeling of which Berman already was well aware.

It was time for a change.

Rick Berman began working on the basic framework of the fifth series long before the *U.S.S. Voyager* made its way home. "About two and a half years ago, the studio came to me and said they were interested in having me create a new series either to overlap with the last half-year of [*Star Trek:*] *Voyager* or to start after *Voyager* ended. I knew that I was not interested in just doing another twenty-fourth-century series. I felt that after [*Star Trek:*] *The Next Generation* and [*Star Trek:*] *Deep Space Nine* and *Voyager,* to just slap another seven characters into a new ship and send it out in the same time period with the same technology and the same attitudes—for me, for the writers, and I think also for the fans, we had done enough.

"My interest in developing another *Star Trek* series was really contingent upon doing something dramatically different. To me, the most logical thing to do was to take the show back a couple of centuries. We had done a wonderful movie in *Star Trek: First Contact.* In the movie we met Zefram Cochrane in the twenty-first century and we saw Earth in a very distraught state. We knew when we made contact with the Vulcans and we had our first warp flight. We also knew that two hundred years later would be Kirk and Spock and *Star Trek.* But what happened during those two hundred years? What happened between those years of despair and renewal and the era of near perfection that existed when the original *Star Trek* series began? So came the thought of placing a show somewhere in between."

With the time period chosen, a whole new vista for storytelling emerged—one that would allow for ideas that Berman and his team had not been able to explore with the more recent incarnations of *Star Trek*. "I felt that with *Deep Space Nine* and *Voyager* we had captains and crews who were not filled with the charm and fun of doing what they wanted to do. They were, in fact, people who were in uncomfortable positions in places where they really didn't want to be. Benjamin Sisko was not crazy about being on Deep Space 9. He was a recent widower who was filled with despair, which he got rid of to a large degree, but this was not a man who was an adventurer in the sense of where the series took him. Kathryn Janeway also was a rather severe character who felt responsible for having nearly two hundred people lost in space for seven years.

"I felt it was really important that we got back to the basics and we got back to where we had a crew that were doing exactly what they wanted to do—who were explorers, who had a captain who was an adventurer and who was lighthearted. A little bit of Captain Kirk and a little bit of Chuck Yeager. And to have a group going off where no man has gone before. And also a group that—because they were more accessible, because they were more contemporary—we could relate to in a lot of ways. If you or I were on a spaceship and suddenly we came upon an inhabited planet, it would scare the shit out of us. I'm not saying we wouldn't be excited. I'm not saying we wouldn't be filled with awe and amazement. But we'd also be terrified, we'd be nervous. We'd have a whole lot of feelings that people like Jean-Luc Picard never had because this was day-to-day work for him. He took a lot of this stuff for granted. This was all fodder for the creation of what I thought was going to be a wonderful new direction to take the series.

"To see the first humans to truly go out where no one has gone before—this seemed very exciting to me. It seemed exciting to me for the reasons I've just said, but also because it would let the fans see all the things that they had come to know as part of *Star Trek* in their infancy. To see them being developed. To see them not working all that right. Which would mean a lot of fun. It would also make our characters seem closer to the present, which would enable them to be a little bit more contemporary, a little bit more human, a little bit more fun."

With the time period chosen and the basic outline formed, Berman took the idea to Paramount, hoping for the green light that would allow him to start assembling his team. "The studio was a little resistant at first," he admits. "There was a question of 'Why not go further into the future?' But we have found that further into the future tends to mean suits that are a little bit tighter and consoles that are a little bit sleeker. And basically, we'd done that. We've done many episodes where we've had to sneak into the future a little bit. It doesn't bring us that much. By going back, it brought us a great deal. Eventually, when the studio embraced the idea, and Brannon was brought into the process, we began developing the characters and eventually the story and the script."

Brannon Braga, co-creator and executive producer, recalls the morning Berman called him from his cell phone while heading to the studio and asked him to help develop the new show. At the time, Braga was co-executive producer on *Voyager*, and he found the concept of going back to the beginning an exciting proposition. Together, the pair started laying out the universe of the twenty-second century.

"What I can tell you is there's no Federation," Braga explains. "Starfleet is very young. It's only been around for a decade or more. There are some vessels flying around, some low-warp ships like cargo vessels. We've got a colony on the moon. We've got a space station around Mars. We've been exploring, but in a very limited way, because we just didn't have the warp capacity to go very far. We've met some other aliens, courtesy of the Vulcans, but we've never bolted out on our own. We've always been under the Vulcans' close watch. We haven't gone that far. So we're itching to go.

"In terms of how close this Earth is to Roddenberry's vision, I think it falls somewhere between now and Kirk's time. Not everything is perfect. I think humanity has gotten its act together to a large degree. I think that war and disease and poverty are pretty much wiped out. But what's important is that the people aren't quite there yet. I don't think these people have fully evolved into the Captain Picards and Rikers."

The direction of the new series was a dramatic departure from previous series, and the producers knew that the difference had to be reflected in the show's name. The question became how to keep it linked to the proud *Star Trek* history while at the same time making it unique. "Since *The Next Generation*, we've had so many

Star Trek entities that were called *Star Trek* 'colon' something." Berman rattles off the list: "*Star Trek: The Next Generation, Star Trek: Deep Space Nine, Star Trek: Voyager, Star Trek Generations, Star Trek: First Contact, Star Trek: Insurrection*—just one after another. Our feeling was to try and make this show dramatically different—which we are trying to do—and that it might be fun not to have a divided title like that. I think if there's any one word that says *Star Trek* without actually saying *Star Trek* it's the word *Enterprise*." And with that, the title was born.

With a concept, theme, and title, the show needed to find its crew. As always, the most integral role is that of the captain. In this case, they created Captain Jonathan Archer (Scott Bakula), a man in his mid-forties; as the script for "Broken Bow" says, "unlike the captains in centuries to come, he exhibits a sense of wonder and excitement" over his new ship and the chance to explore the stars.

With the captain in place, the senior staff fills in down the line. Chief Engineer Commander Charlie "Trip" Tucker (Connor Trinneer), a Southerner who "enjoys using his 'country' persona to disarm people." Tactical Officer Lieutenant Malcolm Reed (Dominic Keating), a "buttoned-up Englishman" with a flair for weaponry. Helmsman Ensign Travis Mayweather (Anthony Montgomery), an African-American "space-boomer" who grew up on a cargo vessel. And Com Officer Ensign Hoshi Sato (Linda Park), an exolinguist described as "a spirited young Japanese woman" with a fear of space travel.

Though the crew complement is set at around eighty humans, the pre-Federation ship does have characters from alien races thrown into the mix, as is the custom for all *Star Trek* series. T'Pol (Jolene Blalock), a "severe yet sensual" Vulcan observer, accompanies the crew on their first mission and later joins on as science officer. And Dr. Phlox (John Billingsly), an "exotic-looking alien with a benevolent smile," just happens to be the most convenient doctor around when Archer is charged with the task of preparing his crew for departure in three days.

As the audience realized long ago, *Star Trek,* though set in a science-fiction universe, is first and foremost a show about characters. These seven characters will now be added to the *Star Trek* family, and the producers can begin to craft their adventures.

"It's always an ensemble on these shows," Braga explains. "But we're not going to concern ourselves, necessarily, with divvying up episodes between characters. The star of this show is the captain and he really will drive the stories, but everyone will be involved. Trip is a major character, and T'Pol is certainly a major character. And the others—it's hard to predict. For instance, the first episode after the pilot, to our surprise, is a big Hoshi episode. It just so happens that that's the show we came up with.

"You can't always predict how it's going to develop over the course of the season. You're also not sure which characters are going to pop out. For instance, I think now we're finding, at least early on, that Trip is really a character that's popping out and with whom we're really having a lot of fun. But, by the end of the season, we could discover that Reed is really jumping off the page. It's hard to say."

Typically, the role of the captain has been the most difficult to fill. The right blend of leadership and compassion are essential if the audience is to connect with the person in the big chair. In this case, according to Berman, the choice was easy from the start. Though the actors cast to play the previous captains of the *Star Trek* series did have followings before being asked on board, Scott Bakula is the most widely known actor to be hired to helm a *Star Trek* series.

Rick Berman explains the benefits of having Bakula sign on. "As a recognized actor he brings a little validity to the show. It doesn't hurt to have someone who is recognizable. I've yet to find people who don't find Scott tremendously talented and likable. When his name was brought up to us by the studio, we jumped for it. We were looking for a little Han Solo quality. We were looking for a little boyishness. We were looking for somebody who had a sense of excitement and awe and was his own man, someone who was young and fit, someone who embodied those heroic qualities that haven't really existed since Captain Kirk. We had a meeting with Scott and just sort of fell in love with him. I cannot think of a single soul I would rather have playing that role."

Once the producers gauged Bakula's interest, casting the rest of the crew became the task at hand. As with any new series, some of the job proved difficult, while some of it was surprisingly easy. "Interestingly, Dominic was someone who read for a role on an episodic show a year before," Berman says. "And I was so impressed with him that—even though it was a year away—I didn't hire him because I thought he'd be great to save for this show. Also, ironically, he was the first actor who came in on the first day of casting."

"The other characters took some time," Braga adds.

"But we eventually found the right people. The hardest role to cast was T'Pol. Anytime you're trying to cast a complex character who's an intelligent, mysterious, complicated alien and also who happens to be a *babe*, it is not an easy task. The last time we really had to do this was with Seven of Nine, and it took a lot of time. So the last role we cast was T'Pol. It took a lot of searching to find that actress who was at once striking and yet had an intelligence about her, who also is a good actress. It is a hard combo, for whatever reason."

Though the search may have been difficult at times, Berman is sure that they have found the perfect crew for *Enterprise*. "I cannot go on more about this cast," he says. "They are extraordinary. I've never been as pleased with putting together a cast of characters as I have with them. Now that we have shot the two-hour pilot and the first episode and are halfway through the second episode, I'm seeing it in every sense."

And as filming progresses through the first season, Berman is excited to see how things develop. "We spent a year and a half creating these characters," he continues. "Then you hire actors to play them. And then, together, these characters are brought to life with both the writing on one side and the actors doing what they do on the other. The characters always—as one season leads to the next—become richer and richer, because there's more and more backstory to them and the actors begin to feel comfortable and they bring unique things to the characters that we as writers and producers would never dream of that are unique to those specific actors."

With the universe and cast firmly in place, the next detail was to lay out the basic themes for the storytelling.

Braga notes that, while the series is deeply entrenched in the excitement of exploration, it will still have its roots closer to home. "We are going to do stories that have ramifications back on Earth," he says. "This is the first ship going out there and they represent humanity. So there are going to be more references to Earth. We are going to deal with certain situations that are closer to Earth and have ramifications closer to home.

"In terms of actually flying the ship back to Earth, that remains to be seen. We haven't decided. I will say that it will not be a frequent thing we'll do, simply because when you're traveling at warp five you get pretty far from Earth pretty fast. To turn all the way around, you're going to have to have a damn good reason. A lot of the pilot takes place on Earth and it's really a fun place to be, strangely enough, because it's kind of a fresh setting for us."

Although the concept for the show took a step back in time, the producers decided to include a bit of a futuristic element as well, adding a shadowed man out of temporal sync with the twenty-second century and a faction of an alien race, known as the Suliban, involved in some mysterious war. Their activities form an intentionally unresolved plotline in the series pilot—part of a story arc the producers hope will continue throughout the life of the series.

"Certain elements came out of discussions that we had with the studio," Berman explains. "We were very impressed with the idea of creating what I like to call a temporal cold war. There are some people from the distant future—maybe as far as the thirtieth century—who have developed time travel. For reasons that we do not understand, there are some people back in the twenty-second century who are doing the bidding of the people from the future.

"Our new breed of bad guys, the Suliban, we learn from the pilot, have been given a great degree of information regarding genetic engineering in exchange for doing the bidding. Why have they come back to the twenty-second century? What is their purpose? Is there one faction from the future? Are there many? We don't know and, in an *X-Files* kind of way, we may not know for years.

"We thought it would be fun," Braga adds, "since this show is a prequel, if we just made it a little bit of a sequel, too. So you have the temporal cold war going on, where factions in the distant future are waging secret battles on various fronts and in various centuries. And the twenty-second century is one of these fronts. We thought it would be interesting to slowly play out a mystery regarding all of this that somehow involves Archer. We're going to be doing that, hopefully, over the course of many, many episodes, possibly seasons. We haven't figured it all out ourselves yet, but we thought that would be a cool idea to layer in."

As for the mysterious man pulling the strings? The script only describes him as "a humanoid figure . . . of indeterminate age." Braga himself is just as cryptic when asked about the man behind the war. "We have several possibilities," he admits. "But we have not settled on any of them and we may come up with yet another one. I think we're going to see how it plays out. . . . We have some ideas, but honestly we don't know for sure. We'll find out along with Archer."

Design

"This new show cannot be just another Star Trek *series. That's really item number one. It will be a ship show, but with an entirely new, entirely different* Enterprise*—one which is both retro and cool at the same time, gritty and utilitarian with space-efficient interior and hands-on equipment. A ship which shows the audience a lot more nuts and bolts than other* Star Trek *series while still having an incredibly futuristic look. In a subtle, very recognizable way, the ship must foreshadow the design of* Enterprises *to come.*

"Chronologically, the drama takes place one hundred years beyond First Contact *and one hundred years before Captain Kirk. Warring factions on Earth have made peace, Starfleet exists, and hundreds of spacecraft of various design have been in use for some time, exploring nearby planets.*

"This Enterprise *is the first spaceship to be filled with the best, to date, Cochrane warp drive—an engine capable of speeds up to warp five. It's a ship with the power to go faster and farther into space than any previous ship*

and to be able to explore planets far outside our solar system."

With those marching orders from Rick Berman, Production Designer Herman Zimmerman began work on what was to become the fifth *Star Trek* series, *Enterprise*—and, more specifically, the *S.S. Enterprise* NX-01. Zimmerman, who served as production designer for two of the *Star Trek* television incarnations—*Star Trek: The Next Generation,* and *Star Trek: Deep Space Nine*—as well as for the more recent films, was excited to have a chance to take a fresh look at the franchise.

"In designing something," Zimmerman says, "you need to have someplace to hang your hat, some philosophy to go on. The first thing that I have to do is, certainly, read the script and be cognizant of the demands of that series on scenes and characters. But also to look further down the line without any actual concrete information as to what might be necessary to flesh out more of the ship than what we're going to see in the first two hours. That's part of the consideration when I start thinking about it."

The production design team must anticipate how each room may be used by this new crew in this new time period. Although, chronologically, this may be the first time a Starfleet crew has manned such a ship, Zimmerman explains, "In the case of *Star Trek,* it's a special kind of vehicle—no pun intended—for storytelling because it has such a rich history."

With his script as a blueprint, Zimmerman began his research. "I do a lot of looking at other science-fiction films," he admits. "While also looking at, particularly in this case, what's current at NASA. What's on the drawing boards for new space shuttles and, again in this case, what's happening in the U.S. military—particularly the Navy, because, as you know, *Star Trek* originated from Roddenberry's interest in the C. S. Forester series of *Horatio Hornblower* novels. The new series has similar models for defining the characters in relationship to each other. That's kind of a *Star Trek* given by this time."

With the series taking place only 150 years from today, Zimmerman made the most logical possible extrapolations of the directions in which he believed the technology will evolve. Then he was able to bridge the gap between spacecraft in current reality and the previously developed *Star Trek* starships of the future. Because, as Zimmerman himself says, "One of our main concerns . . . is to remain true to our position, historically, in the *Star Trek* family."

EXT. SPACE—*ENTERPRISE*

> Our first full view of the majestic ship as it clears the dock and moves into open space. More rocketship than starship, *Enterprise* is lean and masculine—yet its deflector dish and twin warp nacelles suggest the shape of Starfleet vessels to come.

With those lines, the *Enterprise* makes its first full appearance in the script for "Broken Bow." The words on the page, however, fail to convey the full dramatic impact of the ship on the screen. Likewise, they fail to reflect the amount of work it takes to get from the drawing board to the reality.

"The design was originally a different concept entirely than the one with which we ended up," Zimmerman admits. "Which is often the case. You sometimes spend days, weeks, or whatever period of time it takes before the reality sets in, thinking about what you think is the right design for the exterior of the ship, and then someday somebody along the line says, 'Well, that doesn't look very good.' Or in this case, 'Gee, it looks like the old *Enterprise.*' And you realize that you have to go in a totally different direction."

Braga expands on the idea behind the original concept. "I had just gotten back from the LA car show, and I had seen the new 2002 Thunderbird. What I really liked about it was that it was the classic Thunderbird design, but modernized. So it was kind of the best of both worlds. It was at once tantalizingly modern and yet very, very familiar at the same time. So we discussed it and we thought, Well, let's take Kirk's ship, the original *Enterprise,* and let's soup it up and make it more futuristic and bring it into the twenty-first century. And we worked on that for a while, but it ultimately looked just too much like the other ships. It was too familiar. It wasn't new enough. So we ended up completely abandoning that approach and starting from scratch."

"In this case," Zimmerman adds, "we had about a month of sketches and computer-generated images roughly showing shapes of different ships that eventually evolved into a ship that was really cool, but it looked very much like the classic *Star Trek Enterprise.* Now, that was a really cool ship and the series would have been well served by it. But, I don't think it represented what Rick and Brannon see as the vision of this new *Enterprise.* So we went to work again."

Though the producers wanted the look to be different, they did not want it to be so dramatically different that it seemed out of place. This was still to be a *Star Trek* series, which naturally required a *Star Trek* vessel.

Zimmerman describes the path that led them to the new design: "We found a ship that was in our archives—a minor vessel that had been used in a battle in one of the features that had been created by ILM. We did not use that ship, but we took ideas from it and from those ideas eventually—and this process took about four months, all week and weekend CGI work by a very talented Lightwave artist, Doug Drexler—we finally came up with a shape that everybody loves. I trust the fans will love it as well as the producers and the cast do."

"We ended up with a design that is definitely a *Star Trek* vessel in that it has a saucer section and warp nacelles, but it doesn't have an engineering section at the bottom," Braga explains. "It's more shiny and chromelike on its exterior—more metallic and less kind of a flat gray. . . . It's a little bit more like a cross between a stealth plane, a nuclear sub, and a Starfleet vessel."

With the design in hand, the next step in the ship's evolution was to determine the physical aspects of the ship for filming. "The ship as seen on the screen will probably be entirely CGI," Zimmerman says. "There will be models made, but they won't be the principal photography models. We have found, since 1987, that the state of the art has changed dramatically. One of the things that model photography does is give you a very realistic bounce of light. One of the drawbacks of model photography is that you have to build a model for everything. If you have to articulate a torpedo launch mechanism on the exterior of the ship, you have to build it. You have to make it work. And you have to do it in a scale that can be photographed. . . . With the computer-generated images you can be infinitely more flexible. Everything takes time, but once it's built you can look at it in twelve different ways and they'll all be perfect. They'll all be correctly lit. The moves will all be correct for timing and correct for size and shape. All of that is very useful when you're doing a new one-hour episode every seven days—which is what an hour TV show schedule ends up being. So the CGI modeling has come, since 1987, to a state of the art that is not only as good as but better than model photography."

INT. *ENTERPRISE*—BRIDGE

Far more basic than future starships, this command center lacks the "airport terminal" feel of *Enterprise*s A through E. A central captain's chair is surrounded by various stations, the floors and walls are mostly steel, with source light coming from myriad glowing panels. No carpets on the floors, no wood paneling on the walls, high-tech gauges, dials.

Zimmerman recalls his basic direction for the most familiar interior set of all Starfleet vessels. "Rick and Brannon particularly liked two pieces of equipment from the classic *Star Trek* series bridge: Spock's viewer and Uhura's communications earpiece. They thought some earlier versions of these objects might be found to be useful. Well, we did indeed do that, but we did not go so far as to use Uhura's earpiece. It was proven to be an unnecessary device. We did, however, use a modernized, but retro, version of Spock's viewer, and I think the fans will both identify with it and enjoy the connection."

"As far as the interior goes," Berman adds, "we visited a submarine and got the idea of what confined space was like. We tried to make it a little bit more confined but at the same time a hospitable place that the audience would want to come visit every week."

The rest of the set grew out of that directive. Deeper and slimmer than the familiar bridges of *Star Treks* past, the design appears more functional than comfortable, but still warm and inviting. Though the ever-present captain's chair may be the cozy refurbished seat from a Porsche, most of the surrounding chairs are metal mesh and, as Hoshi notes during a particularly rough patch of turbulence, they do not have seat belts to keep the crew strapped in. There are, however, strong metal guardrails encircling the bridge, similar to the one seen in The Original Series, for the crew to clutch on to as they are tossed about.

"It's more hands-on for the crew," Zimmerman says. "There are knobs and buttons and switches and levers and things that actually move and do something. In previous series, since the original—because the original did have buttons to push—we put things behind black plastic. We're now in possession all LCD screens and plasma screens, which are out. We see the frames. There's very little that's built in that's not accessible."

A new addition to the bridge is the set that, in previous series, has proven to be one of the largest challenges to the various *Star Trek* directors. Formerly known as the briefing room, the *Enterprise*'s situation room is set off in an alcove behind the captain's chair but still very much a part of the set. In the past, directors have noted the difficulty in creating interesting scenes within a room that is little more than a large table surrounded by chairs. This new design for the situation room places it in the action rather than away from it and opens up the staging possibilities. Though the space is tight, the room does have removable walls to allow for cameras and lighting, as do all the standing sets.

Another feature in all the sets is the addition of what the production crew refers to as "busy boxes," which Zimmerman describes as "things that can be opened up and worked on during an emergency or even during the routine of getting the ship ready for leaving Spacedock. Leaving so much more for the actors to do."

One familiar set for *Enterprise* is the transporter room. However, the transporters of this earlier time have a bit of a twist. "This transporter is not really recommended for biological organisms," Zimmerman explains. "It's basically a cargo transporter. So while we are occasionally forced to use the transporter for a live specimen, it's not recommended. Mostly we use the shuttles to leave the ship."

This design, too, mixes a little of the familiar with the new. Zimmerman explains, "Again, it's an homage to the Original Series transporter and it's a precursor of all the transporters you've seen since. It's got a single pad, but it does have ribs around it that have the same structural pattern that were on the ribs of the transporter on The Original Series. That was one of the things we did as a nod to Matt Jefferies' designs."

INT. *ENTERPRISE*—MAIN ENGINEERING

Unlike the spacious, brightly lit engine rooms of future starships, this is more like the cramped, red-lit nerve center of a nuclear submarine . . .

A more dramatic change in the design of the interior can be found in the heart of the ship, engineering. Zimmerman's directive for the room was that it be a busy place with lots of moving parts. The concept behind the design is that the room is heat-generating and pulsing. The area is more cramped and the core itself is horizontal, rather than vertical, as were warp cores past.

Zimmerman goes on, "We talked of a honeycomb design with multiple push and pull rods, accessible through openable doors. Machine walls cover the bulk of the engine. In other words, you're not going to see a big roiling mass of energy, you're going to see the result of that through small windows. You're going to see a very powerful engine that looks like a very powerful engine." And the audience will also see the process by which the energy is distributed, through tubes leading out of the core directly to the warp nacelles.

In short, the design for the engine reflects a more simple time. As Zimmerman explains, "It doesn't look like you can't understand it or that it wouldn't break down if all the components weren't working perfectly. So, it's a more realistic propulsion system than the fantastic propulsion system."

Other sets include the armory, loaded with missiles instead of the futuristic photon torpedoes, and the sickbay, which also has a new look.

"I think my favorite set is sickbay," Braga admits. "Obviously the bridge is very cool, but sickbay, to me, really captures a nice flavor of *Enterprise* because it's so different. It looks so believable. It's kind of white, gleaming, with lots of chrome, and it kind of looks like a real hospital, a real futuristic hospital. I think people will be surprised at the departure we've taken there. But it's well worth it."

Knowing the look of the main vehicle, the production team could then move on to its shuttlecraft. The *Enterprise* shuttles will play a more integral role in this series than in series past, because transporter technology is so new. As Zimmerman previously noted, the *Enterprise* transporter platform is technically *approved* for biotransport, but shuttlecraft are still the preferred method of getting the crew from one place to another.

"The shuttle design is almost a direct steal from the shuttles that are being built right now," Zimmerman admits. "The X-33 [Reusable Launch Vehicle] is probably the closest model to the actual shuttlecraft that we are using on *Enterprise*. We feel that reentry vehicles, right now, are as close to state-of-the-art as they're going to be in the next hundred years, mainly because we lack the propulsion system that *Star Trek* has so blithely invented without explaining quite how we acquired all that power. Also, I think that will be a delight to the science-oriented viewer, because it's familiar."

The conflicts of designing a series being filmed over thirty years after The Original Series yet taking place almost one hundred years previous to its setting presented a number of problems in the course of the design. At some point in the planning for each set, prop, costume, and even makeup application, a decision needed to be made on where to bridge the gap—whether to make extrapolations based on current technology or on the vision of the future circa 1967. In the end, a combination of periods was achieved, with the emphasis being on a future based on the technology of today.

The most difficult challenge for maintaining design continuity was the props, since some concessions needed to be made along the lines of the more portable equipment. Considering how far technology has come in the last decade alone, what may have appeared futuristic in the sixties does not hold up to today's technological advancements. According to Berman, the decision on how true to remain to the original needed to be made on a case-by-case basis; as an example, he points out that the computer on his desk is less bulky than the one that sat on Captain Janeway's desk on *Voyager.*

One of the most recognized props from The Original Series was the communicator. The wireless handheld device, so ahead of its time for the original audience of Kirk and Spock, is old hat for today's audience, many of whom have similar devices in their homes, cars, and jacket pockets. Again, Zimmerman was required to bridge the gap between the technology of yesterday's future with today's. "They're quite along the lines of the communicators that we saw in the classic series and the early movies, but, because they are being designed now, they are much cooler and much more interesting pieces of equipment. Their function is pretty much the same. We're not doing badges—we're doing flip-open communicators, tricorders, and other diagnostic equipment that is small. It is microminiaturized, but it is not vastly different in its design from the great things that are being done now."

This quickly became the defining element for all props, Zimmerman admits. "The truth is our props are more capable but less slim and compact than what you can buy today. That's part of the dramatic necessity, so the actor has something that the audience recognizes instantly and that works. Having said that, they are really interesting props and they will make interesting devices for the telling of a story."

And it is those stories that the designs will best serve. "There's a lot of wonder and awe and sense of the first time in all of the concepts for the stories," Zimmerman explains. "This is no 'Ho hum, we're out in space again, we know how to do this. Just sit back and watch us.' It's like we're discovering it for the first time and it's really very exciting. It's reinventing the franchise in many, many ways."

And the designer is just as excited about this new opportunity. "Personally, it's a kick in the right place to get an opportunity to reinvent a *Star Trek* venue like this, because one gets set in one's ways always doing it the same," he continues. "This is so fresh, such a new approach, such an opportunity to go back to the roots of something that you've already done and say, 'Well, how was it that it came to this point? How would it look if it was two hundred or three hundred years before but still in our future and maintained the continuity that eventually leads into Captain Picard and the *Enterprise-E?'* Well, that's a fun job. Why wouldn't you like that?"

Costume designer Robert Blackman started working on *Star Trek* in the third season of *The Next Generation,* and was asked back for the latest installment, ready for his own challenge of reinventing the franchise. To do so, he looked at the series as a whole, focusing first on the evolution of the Starfleet uniform.

"We talked about the *Star Trek* timeline and where [the

series] fit," says Blackman. "We've got original *Star Trek,* we've got the movies, we've got *The Next Generation, DS9,* and *Voyager.* They all travel in a linear direction. We know where we started, originally, with classic *Star Trek,* and we know where we ended, at this point, which is *DS9.* Where those changes for the garments happened were pretty clear. It was then taking that knowledge of how it progressed and working backwards."

The first question naturally became just how far to back up. Blackman's challenge was to determine where the uniform design would have been one hundred years before The Original Series. To do this he chose an approach quite like Zimmerman's approach to the designs for sets and props. Blackman looked to current apparel as his basis for extrapolating a look for the future. "What I chose to do was to back up to now and to do a lot of investigation on, essentially, supersonic jet pilot testing suits, NASA suits, that sort of look, and then play around with those and kind of move forward on them."

Blackman likens his work to the evolution of clothing in general. "It's sort of like the tie, which has been around for a hundred and thirty years and I don't think that people are going to necessarily be tie-less in the next hundred and thirty years. There are aspects that are very familiar to us today that are recognizable aspects. I keep pressing those to really land it closer. We're all well versed in what we imagine life in the universe will be in four or five hundred years, but what it's going to be in a hundred years is another thing. So, my gut response to that is to tie it more to now than to then."

In the case of *Star Trek,* the Starfleet uniforms have

become integral to the look of the series. Blackman explains that the new look is a radical departure from the past. "All of the Starfleet stuff is natural fibers. For the first time ever, there are zippers and pockets. We've never had them. From The Original Series on, they were eliminated. Pockets, because the idea was there was no currency. There was nothing. You didn't need house keys. It was all done electronically. No zippers or buttons because the clothes were imagined to be put on in some sort of way, by forcefield, or whatever the hell you wanted it to be." In fact, the uniforms have taken on a more casual look beyond the addition of pockets and zippers with accessories of utility caps and away jackets.

"They wear black mock turtlenecks underneath," Blackman continues. "The uniforms are a darkish blue, brushed twill that is stonewashed. So they look a little bit worn. There is a whole kind of casualness to it. They're wrinkly. They're just something that is not as formalized as we have done previously. They still are sort of formfit and sleek in the body. All of our people look heroic in them, which is always the goal. So there's always those kinds of things that remain constant."

Among the familiar, however, is the designation of department insignias. "One of the things that we're resonating from the future are the color bars," Blackman adds. "The colors are the same, but they had switched after original *Star Trek* to the movies and then from the movies to *The Next Generation.*" For this new series, Blackman reverted to the original. "What command was, and what security was, and what science was made a change that we have honored. Command positions are gold now, not red. Science is still blue. Security and engineering are red." Then he changed the design, making it an accent to the uniform instead of the focal point. In this case, the insignia is simply a thin stripe that goes around the yoke of the uniform.

Environment is also a consideration for the costumes on the series. Since the characters spend most of their time on the ship, the uniforms must contrast with those sets to some degree. While the overall design is an important consideration, Blackman does not allow it to entirely determine his concepts. "I look to see what the designs are, but the colors of the set don't really influence me in this particular world," he explains. "My notion is that if you have that much activity in the background then you need to make the thing in the foreground, which is usually the actor, as simple as possible. Hence, these sort of blue matte fabric uniforms. Yeah, they've got zippers and so on and so forth, but that does all blend eventually and you're really just looking at the surface. There are a couple of scenes I saw being shot where they're standing in front of a lot of moving graphics and you never lose them. You're never distracted by the graphics. The graphics are brilliant, but they don't talk."

Though the *Enterprise* is an Earth ship with a crew made up almost entirely of humans, two alien characters have been added to the mix in the form of T'Pol, of Vulcan, and Dr. Phlox, of an alien race new to *Star Trek.* These characters represented two distinctly different challenges for Blackman. In T'Pol he has a character of a race the audience is quite familiar with. The task in this case was to maintain the familiar while reinventing the look more for today's audience.

Blackman describes his approach to this new character: "Some of it is about broad-based marketing and other parts of it are about getting a character going. That uniform has a sort of form fit. It's a very beautiful woman. But it has certain things that, over the years, I have distilled out of the original Vulcans. When I say the original Vulcans, I'm talking the return of Spock—the movies' version rather than anything that happened in The Original Series. Those things are very much based on a kind of Chinese silhouette. They were very metallic and very brocadey and flat at the same time. . . . Over the years, I developed a kind of eye that gave you an echo of that. It's a serpentine thing that starts slightly extended from the shoulder point and then curves in and back out so you get the notion that you're creating a very wide shoulder as some of those mandarin clothes do, but without actually doing it. So, that is the basis to her.

"The Vulcan civilization is also X amount of years earlier. She's definitely in earth tones. It's kind of a gray/brown, very sort of striated piece of fabric. The Vulcans tend to be more coolish in color. I've chosen not to do that. I've chosen to warm her up. She plays against it. She's very Vulcan in the script and she's very Vulcan—and will be, I think—throughout. There's a hint of Vulcan in the design and it's got to be a uniform. We've never seen the Vulcans in uniform before. So I just went with this other look."

On the other hand, there is Dr. Phlox, a character from a distinctly new race of what the script refers to only as "an exotic alien species." As there was no *Star Trek* history to look to for his specific character, Blackman started with a basis in familiar Earth design and evolved from there. He describes the look as similar to shirts of East Indian design that tend to be longer and hang down over the pants. Blackman goes on, "I've taken that design—using that as a kind of gentle shape—to pull him away from the rest of the people. These sort of shirt/smock things. And then just added a few odd details to them so that they are very alien to all of the Starfleet stuff that you see, but they're not so alien that you don't forget about it soon, and he just becomes a guy with a really benevolent face."

Another aspect of the design for the series is the more casual tone of an earlier time in Starfleet. To set this tone, Berman has said, the audience will see the crew out of uniform from time to time. Where the concept of the uniform is important, however, Blackman admits that it is the civilian clothes that can prove the larger challenge. "In any of the timeframes, those have always been the more difficult clothing to do. It's just hard to figure out what it is. You get to a uniform or something that is really extreme, then it's easy. You can just make it really extreme. I always sort of hark back to *The Fifth Element.* You look at that and you go, Okay, there are backless T-shirts with straps across them. But we can't go that far. It's not our world. So you'll see Captain Archer in the first two episodes in essentially T-shirts and jean-cut pants with odd shoes. It is a gentle nod to the future with a fairly strong stance in the present."

Also making an appearance in the pilot episode is one of the favorite *Star Trek* races, the Klingons. And with the new setting, an earlier version of this race needed to be defined as well. Of course, makeup applications have come a long way since the sixties. These Klingons will appear more as they do in the later versions of *Star Trek*—a look that had its inception in the film *Star Trek: The Motion Picture* and grew into the Klingons of modern *Star Trek*. Though the appearance may be modern, however, the concept of the race will be entirely fresh.

"The Klingons are to a degree 'proto-Klingons,' " Braga explains. "They're Klingons that come long before the Klingons of Picard's time. Therefore they can be gnarlier, nastier, more warlike Klingons than ever. They'll eat the hearts of their victims and sharpen their teeth and so forth."

This description led Blackman to a very specific look. "It's very rough furs and leathers and chain-maily," he explains. "They still have the kind of boots that we're used to, though nothing is black and gray anymore. It's all kind of earth tone. They're pretty dirty. They look pretty ratty, really. But that was the deal, so it's more primitive than we have seen before."

Another key element to the show will be the ongoing temporal cold war. The foot soldiers of that war in the twenty-second century are the new race of *Star Trek* aliens known as the Suliban. "There are two different groups in the same time period," Blackman explains. "Kind of the good Suliban and the bad Suliban. The bad ones are like chameleons. They are genetically mimetic. They can mimic or become anything they need to. It is not the same as a shapeshifter. Their skin will turn into whatever it needs to turn into. Consequently the bad ones have developed that technique to the point where they can manufacture it. So they have manufactured this as part of their clothing and are then able to change themselves, physically, and their clothing, physically. The good ones haven't done that, or if they have that capability, they don't use it. So they appear in things that are definitely futuristic, but don't relate to their skin."

With these aliens, Blackman worked closely with makeup designer Michael Westmore, as much of the look of the aliens is mirrored in their clothing. "The characters have a very specific, kind of peculiar, skin, which we were able to copy in a pretty good way," Blackman explains. "It's a different color, but when you see them, the skin texture and the texture of the clothing are very reminiscent of one another. They are pretty much very simple jumpsuits with built-in feet. They're just colored this amazing color and they're very slight of stature."

Blackman looks forward to the challenges of the new series, especially because they are *new*. "I think it would have been more daunting and more difficult if the spin that I had to do was to take what I had done over twelve years and split that hair one more time," he explains. "That would have been a really difficult thing. The difficulty here was not really coming up with the ultimate look—the appearance of the uniform—it was the process of evolving that. It required quite a few completely rendered prototypes to get us to say, 'No, no, we don't want it to be a weird synthetic fabric. No, we want it to have a more now, today, this moment, look.' So that was the process that was hard. And that's the process that's hard every day as regards this series right now. We don't have much of a frame of reference for it. So, we're continually reinventing that or inventing that. That becomes the difficulty. But the difficulties kind of get your head in the right place to be able to do it."